MISTAKE CREEK

RACHEL AMPHLETT

SAXON
PUBLISHING

ONE

Central Valley, California

Kyle Roberts sucked in a deep breath of air and willed the fire in his leg muscles to ease.

He'd been running for what seemed an age, sliding over exposed stones and rocks, all the time straining his ears to listen for signs of his pursuers.

His jeans, dirty and torn, stuck to his legs, the ends of his shirt flapping from under a faded black leather jacket.

He stopped and squinted over his shoulder, paranoia squeezing his gut.

Intermittent flashes of lightning illuminated the landscape, casting an eerie purple-yellow hue across the terrain. Clouds tumbled over each other, hastening towards the valley, churning the sky into darkening shades of grey.

They'd heard the storm warnings on the radio earlier that afternoon – news of a drought-breaker, with the accompanying instructions to secure loose outdoor items and seek shelter.

The men had worked more urgently, the whole team desperate to keep the operation on schedule. Tempers had frayed, his real identity had been compromised, and then Kyle had found out what it was like to be on the receiving end of a sharp knife.

His hand traveled to his shoulder and came away sticky. The wound would never stop bleeding all the time he remained in motion, but he had little choice.

He ran a dirty hand through his hair and wondered if John had managed to get away from the men who wanted them dead, whether he was now steering the stolen car along the dirt track that ran between the farming properties across the ridge towards town.

They'd heard rumours that the creek had been likely to flood, taking out the bridge that spanned the wide expanse of water, and in turn wiping out any hope they'd held to get help.

They'd only managed to escape with one vehicle, Kyle choosing to jump out and send John on his way while he escaped on foot in the opposite direction, hoping to distract their pursuers.

If he did make it as far as the highway without being caught, Kyle planned to flag down the first available vehicle and disappear in the opposite direction, over the range and away from the valley.

He'd ruled out heading to the neighbouring farm to raise the alarm – their pursuers would likely check there first.

Trouble brewed over his shoulder, in the shape of an angry grey and purple storm front. The storm head billowed towards him, darkening the skies, while the rocky escarpment beyond had become a blue-grey hue.

A flock of birds screeched overhead, their route taking them away from the encroaching onslaught.

The air had turned oppressive, viscous with charged ozone and a stifling humidity. On the horizon, patches of pale sunlight shone through the grey clouds, attempting a last stand against the approaching storm.

Fat raindrops hit the ground, the coolness hissing against the hot earth.

His head twitched as, to his left, half a mile below him on the incline, a dark shape lurched forwards through the gloom and began to gain height, the far-off roar of a powerful engine reaching his ears.

They were closing in on him.

He gritted his teeth and swore in frustration as his waterlogged boots sank into the mud, slowing him down. He wrenched his foot from the soaked earth and began to stagger towards the upper part of the ridge. With any luck, he'd be able to get his bearings from there, rather than struggling over the landscape with little sense of direction. He had to concentrate, to act on his survival skills and cunning, if he was going to survive the next few hours and complete his mission.

He paused, plunged his hand into his pocket, and pulled out a cell phone. Holding it up, he spun round trying to get a single bar of signal to appear at the top of the screen.

'Come *on*,' he urged, before turning in a different direction and trying again.

He had to warn them, to tell them he'd failed, that what they had been so desperately trying to prevent was happening, *now*.

A strangled curse of frustration escaped his lips. Either the incoming electrical storm had scrambled the signal, or the emergency services were receiving so many calls from people living in the valley that the service was overloaded.

In any event, he wasn't going to be making a phone call any time soon.

He swore under his breath. Everything about the plan had turned to shit. He'd spent six months setting it up, but his plan hadn't factored in the possibility that he'd be stabbed trying to prevent a catastrophe from taking place, or that a drought-breaking storm would descend on the valley, sending his target into a panic.

He snorted at the irony, began to put the phone back in his pocket, and then shouted in alarm as the ground gave way under his feet.

He lashed out with his arms and legs to slow his

descent, swore as the branch of a tree sapling whipped his cheek, and then slid to a halt, breathing hard.

The hairs on the back of his neck stood on end. He lay still for a moment, letting the rain wash the blood from his torn face and hands while he caught his breath, before he hauled himself up into a crouching position. He strained his ears to hear above the pounding of the rain, trying to get his bearings.

His hand moved to his pocket, and he closed his eyes as he realized what had happened.

He'd lost the phone.

He raised his eyes to the tracks of his fall and searched the undergrowth, moving swiftly, left to right across the path of destruction his body had made as he'd fallen.

Nothing.

He clasped his hands over his head and pivoted in a circle, cursing.

He glanced over his shoulder. The top of the ridge was now even further away from him, the tracks of his fall evident in the next blinding flash of lightning that swept across the darkening sky and illuminated the stark landscape. He couldn't afford to waste time. If the phone was gone, then he *had* to escape. It was the only way.

An engine revved, its throaty roar filling the air.

He spun round, searching in all directions, trying to pinpoint his pursuers.

The hillside exploded with light as headlight beams

criss-crossed the ground in front of him. Spotlights swept the mist, seeking him out.

They'd split up, trying to catch him in a classic pincer movement.

He turned and ran.

Behind him, he heard a shout, and then the vehicle changed gear and began its pursuit.

He weaved across the rugged hillside, grabbing tree branches and exposed rocks to work his way higher, away from the vehicle.

His leg muscles aching from the swift ascent, he sucked in air as he reached the summit.

He hauled himself over the edge, and saw the lights of the small town in the distance where, only three days ago, he'd ventured into the camping store for supplies. Through the gloom, the sickly orange glow of halogen streetlights bobbed in and out of view between swaying trees as the prevailing wind lashed the surrounding countryside.

He groaned – it was too far.

He checked over his shoulder.

Below, the pursuit vehicle steadily moved across the ridge, gaining on him, the whine of its engine carrying over the wind as it climbed towards him, and then stalled.

Kyle turned his attention back to the valley below. He was running out of time. He could only hope that John had made it to the highway, and that the creek hadn't burst its banks before he'd made it into town.

He squinted at the road leading from the town up to the

ridge, where it joined the main highway. No traffic moved except for a single headlight beam, and he frowned, wondering if the run-off from the surrounding water catchment had already burst the creek's banks and blocked the road.

A faint light towards the bottom of the ridge caught his eye, and he shielded his eyes from the rain and squinted. In the next flash of lightning that shot across the valley he saw a low-set building with some sort of canopy at the front.

He wracked his memory until he remembered a run-down truck stop, a 'for sale' sign across its front window.

Adrenaline surged through his body as he realized he'd have to make a run for it and pray the building still had a working telephone.

The tree trunk next to him exploded a split second before he heard the gunshot reverberate in his ears.

He threw himself to the ground and began to crawl away on his elbows and knees, keeping his head down.

The vehicle's engine roared to life again, the headlights seeking him out. He scrambled up and slid down the ridge towards the valley, ducking behind trees and boulders.

He tripped and curled up as he fell, gritting his teeth as sharp stones dug into his back before he slowed to a stop. He eased himself up onto all fours and lifted his head.

The vehicle crested the ridge above him before it braked to a standstill. The driver's door swung open, and a figure stepped out into the rain.

Kyle groaned, his lungs aching from the exertion, and watched, helpless, while the figure leaned into the cab of the four-wheel drive and emerged, holding a rifle.

'You should've stayed away,' yelled the figure. 'You should've minded your own damn business.'

'I was,' he murmured.

He jumped sideways as the rifle bucked once in the figure's hands, and then everything went black.

TWO

'Nina, let me do that – you're going to fall.'

'I'll be okay. Keep your foot on the ladder and stop staring at my backside.'

'It's hard not to. It's right in my face.'

'Hold on to the ladder and keep your eyes lowered, Ross.'

She ignored the laugh below her, the rich tones filling the air. Instead, she slid the tarpaulin over the last of the loose tin panels, adjusted her balance on the ladder, and fired the nail-gun, sealing the plastic sheeting into place.

'Okay, we're all done on this side.'

She glanced behind. Already, the wind was picking up, shaking the corn stalks in the fenced-off field on the opposite side of the road.

She changed her grip on the nail-gun and then

9

descended the length of the ladder. As she reached the bottom, Ross stood aside, one hand gripping the frame. She smiled up at him. 'See, I'm quite capable.'

'Oh, I know that.' He pushed his hat back on his head, his green eyes sparkling. 'But I'll bet this side comes unstuck the moment that storm hits, whereas the *other* side will be fine.' He grinned. 'That'll be the side I sorted out, of course.'

He laughed and took a step back as Nina aimed a playful punch at his arm. 'Too slow, Nina O'Brien. Way too slow.'

Nina ran a hand through her hair and raised her gaze to the roof. 'Seriously, Ross – do you think it'll be okay?'

'Time will tell. You're doing all you can.' He bent and gathered up the pile of folded plastic sheets. 'Come on, one more to do.' He snatched the nail-gun from her hand and passed her the last tarpaulin. 'And *I'll* go up the ladder this time.' He lowered the ladder and swung it over his shoulder.

The sound of a hammer against wood echoed off the nearby accommodation block.

Nina and Ross had been joined half an hour ago by Phil Allison. A long-distance truck driver, Phil had dropped off a delivery in town and had decided to call it quits for the day after hearing about a landslide that had blocked the highway leading out of the valley and through the hills towards the city. A regular customer of Nina's father's, Phil had been only too happy to stop and help in return for free overnight accommodation.

Now, he was helping them prepare the property for the worst, boarding up windows on the other side of the truck stop and removing anything that could be whipped up by the wind and cause damage.

As the storm had progressed southwards towards Mistake Creek, it had swelled rivers and streams, waterlogging the topsoil until it weakened and collapsed, pulling trees and scrubby undergrowth with it.

As Nina walked, she took in the state of the building, the paint peeling, and the accommodation block that would need tidying up – if the property didn't get ravaged by the incoming storm. A groan escaped her lips.

'Are you okay?' asked Ross, concern creasing his brow.

'I keep seeing more stuff that needs sorting out before I can sell this place. It's never-ending.'

'On the plus side, that means you stay longer.'

'Maybe,' said Nina. 'I need to concentrate on finding a new job and getting Dad's treatment sorted out first.'

Ross started walking again. 'Well, you're better off out of the city anyway. You could do with a bit of country air to put some color in your face. You look as pale as a vampire.'

'Some would say pale and interesting, you know.'

'Is that right? What – just after they order a chai latte or whatever?'

Nina shook her head as she followed him. He still insisted on wearing the battered brown felt hat her father had given him the last year he and Nina were in school together, although its edges were frayed, the shape only just held together by the contours of his head.

She'd told him three days ago when she'd first arrived that her trip here had to be brief. Her job loss had been a blow, and she had to find a new employer fast. She'd calculated that her meagre savings gave her enough time to make any necessary repairs to the truck stop, put it on the market, and cross her fingers that it sold quickly so that she could pay her father's medical bills.

She let her gaze drift to the back of Ross's head. He'd changed a lot since she'd left. Hell, they'd *both* changed a lot. In Ross's case, the lanky awkward farmer's son had gone. In his place stood a man who seemed strong, capable, and definitely good-looking.

Ross dropped the tarpaulin and the nail-gun on the ground before swinging the ladder off his shoulder. Once he had set it straight on the ground, he handed the nail-gun to Nina.

'Okay, pass that and a tarp up when I get to the top.' He looked over her head. 'That storm's moving fast.'

'Will your place be okay?'

He nodded. 'Dad's got Tim, and a couple of the hired hands stayed to help them before they headed home.' He raised his gaze. 'And our roof is in a *lot* better condition than yours, it has to be said.'

12

Nina held on to the sides of the ladder as he climbed, the frame swaying under his weight. She stood on tiptoe, passed him the nail-gun, and then let her mind wander as he worked, the punch of the steel tacks beating a rhythm to her thoughts.

The Flanagan property was a twenty-minute drive from where she stood. Growing up, Ross and his younger brother Tim were the nearest neighbours to her home, often saving a space for her on the school bus as it belched fumes and idled at the now-derelict bus stop opposite the truck stop, the driver impatient as she'd hurried towards it, before continuing its onward journey into the town a further eight miles up the road.

As soon as he'd heard the storm warning on the radio, Ross had driven over to her father's truck stop, his pick-up truck laden with wooden planks and spare tarpaulins. They'd spent the morning boarding up the large floor-to-ceiling windows, moving the old plastic outdoor furniture into one of the dilapidated storage sheds behind the property, and removing anything that could become a missile in the height of the storm.

Nina lifted her face and inhaled. The tang of ozone filled her senses as a low rumble of thunder resonated in the distance. She jumped at the sound of Phil's voice breaking into her reverie.

'You've got plenty of fuel for the generator, right?'

She frowned and bit her lip. 'I checked batteries, torches, candles, and matches. I didn't see any fuel cans.'

Ross snorted. 'It'd be kind of ironic if the only truck stop for miles ran out of petrol for its own generator.'

'Dad hasn't sold petrol for weeks, Ross – you know that.'

'Yeah. Sorry.'

None of them mentioned the incident that had put paid to the possibility of her father continuing to run the business – and nearly killed him in the process.

Nina moved to one side as a swathe of plastic rippled above her head. 'You okay up there?'

'Almost done.'

Nina held the ladder while it wobbled under Ross's weight. She took a step back as he joined her at ground level.

Wiping a bead of sweat from his forehead, he peered up at the black clouds tumbling towards them. 'We should have a final walk around to make sure we've got everything covered.'

Phil began to pick up the leftover planks of wood they'd been using to board up the windows around the building.

'I'll get these stowed away in the barn,' he said. 'Last thing you need is the wind getting hold of them.'

'Great, thanks. Put a couple by the back door, though, in case we need to do running repairs.'

Nina led Ross back to the front of the property. The two fuel bowsers stood sentinel under a steel-framed canopy, dust obliterating the faded logos that covered their surfaces. The oil company had sent out a mechanic and driver to remove the hoses and drain the tanks within days of her father's enforced decision to close the business. At the thought of the tanker truck pulling out of the dirt courtyard and onto the main road for the last time, she fought back tears.

Ross had told her yesterday that he'd driven across to be with her father at that time. The older man had scowled and grumbled about the mess the mechanic had made of the courtyard and the paltry sum of money the oil company had sent him for the recovered fuel. Afterwards, he'd sat in the old wooden rocking chair next to the front door, lost in thought, only raising a hand in farewell when Ross's vehicle pulled away.

Nina shook her head, the reality of selling the place where she'd grown up hitting her harder than she liked to admit. Although she knew it wasn't a home like some people's, it had been one to her.

'Hey.'

The soft tones of Ross's voice interrupted her thoughts. She wiped her fingers across her eyes. 'I'm okay, really, I am.'

He reached out and rubbed her arm. 'It was always going to be tough coming back here, Nina.'

'Yeah.'

She sniffed and shifted the weight of the tools in her arms. 'Come on – before I feel the need to aim that nail-gun at something.'

Ross grinned. 'Atta girl.'

Nina looked up as the first raindrops hit the tin roof, wet splashes striking the dirt unprotected by the building's canopy. She blinked as forked lightning lit up the furthest edge of the weather front, and the rain began to fall in earnest.

With the truck stop bordered by a creek bed six miles away in the direction of town and only the one paved road twisting and narrow in the other direction now blocked by a landslide, she could be stranded for a number of days.

'Remind me to check the cupboards for food supplies,' she said as they hurried to shelter under the canopy. 'And water.'

'Right. Although I don't think you're going to have time to get to town and back for supplies now. If you're worried, we could always drive over to my place in the morning. Dad and Tim would love to see you.'

The rain fell harder, gathering momentum as thunder shook the hills surrounding the property, pelting the fibreglass roof over their heads.

'That'd be nice.' Nina rubbed her hands over her eyes to clear the water that was running through her hair and onto her face, before squinting through the deluge of rain that cast a mist through the valley. She glanced over her shoulder and frowned. 'Hey – look at that.'

She pointed along the road behind, its winding path leading back along the valley towards the ridge in the distance. A single headlight beam shone through the gloom.

Ross held on to his hat as the wind tried to lift it off his head. 'Someone's in a hurry, aren't they?' He hefted the ladder onto his shoulder. 'I'm going to get this put away and make sure Phil's got everything else sorted out.'

'Okay,' said Nina as he walked away, before she slipped a spare elastic band off her wrist and tied her long black strands into a loose ponytail.

She watched the motorbike as it drew level with the truck stop, the engine now audible over the onslaught of rain, and then it shot past, heading towards town, its two passengers hunkered low in their seats.

Ross reappeared and joined her under the shelter of the canopy, his shirt soaked, water dripping from his hat.

Nina noticed how his wet shirt clung to his chest before clearing her throat, and then her attention was caught by a flash of lightning as it zig-zagged across the purple clouds. Long arching trails of blinding white light flickered against the darkening sky. A thick curtain of rain blanketed her view of the ridgeline as it descended towards the valley.

A gust of wind blew under the canopy, and Nina rocked on her feet to keep her balance. 'I think we'd better move inside.'

'Good idea.'

She led the way into the shop area of the truck stop. Empty shelves lined the walls, and an old threadbare sofa nestled in a space between them where she and Ross had pulled it from the living area. She'd managed to sell the commercial refrigerators last week to an interstate business. The owner had haggled over the price with her until she'd simply given in, too exhausted to argue with the man.

A counter encircled one back corner of the room, where her father had set up the till and the coffee-making facilities. In later years, he'd acquired a liquor licence to sell beer and spirits, but only once the authorities had sent a representative out to check that he had accommodation facilities on site.

She crossed the tiled floor, working through lists in her head. What to sell, what needed to be cleaned, and what needed to be repaired – or thrown into the huge trash bin outside that was already overflowing under a tarpaulin.

Ross and Phil flicked switches on panels lining the walls, and the overhead lights came on, illuminating the space in a dull yellow hue.

Bright light flashed through the front door, a loud rumble shaking the building.

Now inside, they could hear the radio, the excited tones of the announcer warning about the landslide, heavy rain, and flash flooding of the creek caused by run-off from higher areas already soaked by the deluge, before static hissed and spat through the airwaves, obliterating his voice.

Ross threw his hat onto the counter and ruffled his hair before peeling his shirt off and hanging it over a chair.

She turned away. He hadn't said anything yet, but she wondered how Ross felt about her being back after so many years. Since her arrival, they'd been so busy making lists and working through what needed to be done before the truck stop was put up for sale, they'd had no time to talk properly.

With the storm fast approaching, and Phil's presence, it was unlikely they'd get that chance any time soon.

Nina moved to the window next to the front door and peered through the gaps in the wooden boards she and Ross had finished nailing into place earlier that afternoon. The strength of the wind outside buffeted against the glass, and she felt the pulse of its energy through the panes.

She frowned as a light shone through the exposed glass that they'd left to use as a peep-hole.

The two men wandered across to stand with her as the throaty roar of a motorbike engine rumbled to a halt outside.

'Sounds like we're going to have more company,' said Nina, and opened the door.

'They must've decided it was too risky to keep going,' agreed Phil.

Outside, a woman was dismounting the pillion seat of a large adventure motorbike while a man switched off the engine and removed his helmet.

The woman slipped her helmet off, brushed her fingers through her hair, and hurried towards Nina.

'Can you help us?' she said, her voice taut. 'We were trying to get into town but this weather, it's just…'

'Of course, we can. Come in.' Nina stood back as the diminutive blonde stepped over the threshold, and guessed her to be in her forties. She started at the sight of the man as he followed.

Older, perhaps in his fifties, he had hair clipped close to his head, silver in color. He towered over Nina, and she realized he was taller than Ross. A small scar ran from his brow to his hairline above his left eye.

As he drew closer, his gaze met Nina's, and his eyes narrowed before he seemed to catch himself. A split second later, his face transformed as he smiled, walked into the truck stop, and pushed the door shut.

'Thanks,' he said, and turned to them. 'I wasn't sure whether anyone was here.' He glanced over at the woman. 'Although I think we should've pushed on into town.'

Ross stepped forward next to Nina and made the introductions.

'Sean,' said the motorcyclist. 'And this is Dani.'

The woman shook hands, then peeled off her leather jacket and draped it over a chair.

'I still say that we'd be fine on the bike,' said Sean, frowning at the gesture.

'Is everything okay?' asked Nina.

'I'm trying to convince my wife that we should keep moving.'

A loud rumble of thunder rolled around the sky outside.

'Listen,' said Nina. 'I know it might seem an inconvenience – it's pretty basic after all – but trust me, stay here.' She moved along the counter, gathered the tools, and placed them on the floor out of the way. 'That storm sounds like it's moving on, but from what we've been hearing on the weather reports, this is only the start of it. It's going to get pretty rough out there.'

Sean held up his hand. 'I'm sorry – I didn't mean to sound ungrateful for your hospitality.'

'No offence taken.'

'It's just that, well, we were hoping to be further along on our journey by now.'

'Where have you been staying?' asked Ross.

'We tried sheltering at the Hudson property but decided to press on.'

Ross laughed. 'I'd have been surprised if he'd let you stay there; he's not known for his hospitality.' He turned to Nina. 'I got a new neighbour three years ago – he's a bit strange and tends to keep to himself. He doesn't even take part in any of the community events held in town.'

The motorcyclist nodded. 'It was a bit awkward, so we made our excuses after half an hour and left.'

'As long as it's not putting you out of your way, us being here?' Dani's hopeful expression belied her words.

'You're better off waiting it out,' said Phil. 'It must be a bad weather front – all I had on the radio coming through the valley was static.' He held up his cell phone. 'I can't even get a signal on this.'

'Which would make it impossible for anyone to help you if you did get into trouble,' added Nina. She jerked her head towards the telephone fixed to the wall behind the counter. 'Our landline's out too.'

'She's right,' said Ross. 'Wait it out in the dry.' He peered through the door at the motorbike parked next to the building. 'I'd hate to see a beautiful machine like that ruined in this weather.'

Sean sighed. 'True. And thanks again,' he said to Nina.

'Let's move your bike now, before it gets worse out there,' said Ross, putting his shirt back on. 'We can put it in the barn – there's plenty of room, and it'll stay dry.'

Nina watched the two men push through the front door; then she turned to Dani, who had reached into her bag, pulled out a compact case, and was fussing with her hair and checking her cell phone for a signal. She glanced up when she realized she was being watched.

'I don't want to sound rude,' she said, 'but I don't suppose there's any chance of a hot drink, is there? I'm freezing.'

'Sure. We'd just finished boarding up the place when the storm hit, so I'll make some coffee for everyone.'

Nina pushed through a gate in the counter and made

her way towards the small kitchen built between the business end of the building and the accommodation.

The old fluorescent lights stuttered before flickering to life, and as she waited for the kettle to boil, Nina began to forage through the cupboards. By the time the hot water was ready, she'd made a small pile on the kitchen counter consisting of cookies, nuts, and dried fruit to sustain them through the night. To this, she added six more candles and a box of matches she'd overlooked while hunting through the cupboards earlier that afternoon.

She walked back to the front of the building with a tray of steaming mugs balanced in her hands and handed out the coffee to everyone as Ross and Sean returned.

As Dani took hers, she thanked Nina again. 'You're sure this isn't too much hassle for you? I feel like we're imposing.'

'Stay with us,' said Nina. 'I'd only worry if you left now.' She jumped as a loud crash of thunder shook the building.

'Jesus, this is going to be rough,' said Ross.

A look of relief passed across Dani's face as the vibration subsided.

Nina walked towards the front door. 'Well,' she said, slipping the bolt across the door, 'now that's settled, I'd be a really bad hostess if I didn't offer you some food, although I warn you, there's not much...'

A loud hammering on the front door startled her, and she spun to face it.

The hammering continued, and she turned to Ross.

He moved across to her, and then shot the bolt back.

Nina cried out as a man collapsed across the threshold, soaked through to the skin, blood covering his face and shoulder. She crouched down, ignoring the rain driving in through the opening, and gently turned the man's face towards her.

'Help me,' he said, and passed out.

THREE

Nina stared at the blood covering her hands and then up at Ross, her mouth open.

'What do we do?'

'Come on – we need to get him inside. Hurry.' Ross coaxed her out of the way, slammed the door shut on the driving wind and rain, and then beckoned to Phil. 'Help me carry him.'

Nina stood on shaking legs against the wall as the two men grabbed the injured stranger under his arms.

'On three. Go!' instructed Ross.

He and Phil lifted the man, both struggling with the dead weight, and carried him through the building.

The stink of mud, sweat, and dirty clothing hung in the air.

'Which spare room is made up?' Ross called over his shoulder.

'They're not,' said Nina, her voice shaking. 'You'll have to put him in my room.'

Dani stood to one side to let the men pass, covering her nose with her sleeve as they staggered past her.

Nina saw that Ross's face had drained of color and realized he was as shocked as her. He appeared to be coping by taking charge of the situation though, and she tried to follow his lead.

She followed them, her mind racing. 'Do you know who he is?'

Ross shook his head. 'Doesn't look like a local. What about you, Phil?'

'No,' said Phil. 'I've never seen him before.'

'I'll grab some towels or something,' said Nina. 'I think there's a first aid kit somewhere.'

'We're going to need it. Have you got some antiseptic or iodine – anything like that?'

'I don't know – I'll take a look.'

She ignored the two men as they lurched through the door into her makeshift bedroom and instead pushed past Dani and Sean with a muttered apology and made her way to the kitchen.

Dani appeared in the doorway. 'Is there anything we can do?'

'I don't think so, unless you know first aid?'

'I'm not very good at dealing with blood.'

'Best sit down, then,' said Nina. 'Last thing we need is for you to faint.'

26

Dani slipped away from the doorway, and Nina resumed her frantic search.

She wrenched open cupboard doors, spilling their contents onto the floor in her haste to locate medical supplies. She pulled out some latex food preparation gloves on her first hunt, and then found a box of sticking plasters.

'We're going to need something bigger than that,' she cursed, and threw the packet across the counter in disgust. 'Christ, is there nothing in this place?'

She spun on her heel, hands on hips, trying to remember where her father kept his first aid kit, and then dashed towards the laundry. Pulling open a cupboard door, she pushed washing powder and fabric conditioner to one side until she located a plastic box.

'Got you.'

She ran back to her room with it.

As she entered, the smell of blood and sweat made her instantly recoil. She groaned when she saw the two men had placed the stranger on her bed instead of the floor, before she shook her head to clear the thought. She handed a pair of the gloves to Ross.

'Put these on. They're better than nothing,' she said. 'And here's the first aid kit. That's everything.'

'Towels?'

'Over in the wardrobe. I'll grab some clean water from the bathroom, hang on.'

When she returned, Phil had moved so he was standing

beside the door, arms folded across his chest, his face grey.

Sean stood next to Ross, his jaw clenched as he watched him roll the man onto his side.

'You might want to go and check on Dani,' said Nina to him. 'She looked a bit pale.'

'Thanks, will do.'

He hurried in the direction of the front room.

Ross glanced up when Nina joined him, slipping gloves over her hands.

'His shoulder's a mess. Help me get this shirt off him and we'll clean him up a bit – see if we can find out what he's done.'

'Okay.'

Phil blew out his cheeks, tugged at his earlobe, and moved towards Ross, his voice low.

'Hate to say it, but that sure looks like a knife wound to me.'

Nina stared at him. 'How can you tell?'

'Seen something like it before,' he said, then shrugged. 'A long time ago.'

'Well, the sooner we get him cleaned up, the better,' said Ross. 'Phil, do you want to go and keep our other guests company?'

'Sure.'

Ross winked at Nina as the other man drifted off along the passageway. 'I think he was going to faint if we'd made him stay any longer.'

'I thought I was going to for a moment there,'

admitted Nina. She pulled away the jacket they'd cut from him and threw it onto one of the chairs next to the bed. She cast a wary gaze over the stranger as she began to cut away at his torn shirt with the scissors. 'Who do you think he is?'

'I don't know.' Ross frowned. 'He looks like he's been living rough, by the state of his clothes. Lots of dirt under his fingernails – hasn't shaved in a while.'

'Do you think Phil's right, that this is a knife wound?'

'Hard to tell – the skin's torn up pretty badly, but if he's had a fall, he might've ripped it open that way.'

'Help me here – I need to peel this material back.' Nina made room for Ross next to the injured man and carefully lifted the shirt cloth away from the man's shoulder. She shuddered as the material peeled back with a wet, tearing noise.

'Gently,' murmured Ross, and helped her lift the man's arm. 'Can you cut this back section away? It might be easier than trying to lift him out of it.'

Nina bent over and cut away the fabric, slipping the loose ends away from the man's body. 'There.'

They both leaned back in shock. Nina flinched at the sight of the wound and looked away.

'Jesus,' swore Ross.

Nina swallowed hard, fighting down the urge to leave the room, and stepped away, closing her eyes to regain her composure.

'You alright?'

She nodded and turned back to Ross. He had his arm across his nose and mouth, his eyes wide.

'I'll be okay. We need to help him, right?'

He nodded and took a deep breath before speaking. 'Okay, warm water first. Let's try to get the dirt off.'

Nina grabbed one of the towels and snipped it into sections before dropping the scissors on the bedside table and soaking the sections of material in clean water.

'How do we know this isn't hurting him?'

Ross's gaze flickered over the man. 'He's out for the count, Nina. Better to do this now than wait for him to wake up, don't you think?'

She nodded, bit her lip, and began work. As she swabbed away the dirt and grit, she couldn't help but sneak the occasional look at the man's face.

His torso and arms were muscular, so he either spent time in the gym or had a job where hard physical labour was a major part of his role.

Nina wiped the dirty water away from his body, ignoring the fact that her sheets and mattress would be ruined by the time they finished.

She looked over her shoulder to see Ross rummaging through the plastic box of medical supplies.

He caught her looking as he held a small bottle up to the light and grimaced. 'I don't think some of this stuff has been opened for years.'

'Do you think it'll be okay to use?'

He shrugged. 'It's going to be better than nothing.' He

put the box down and approached the bed, an assortment of bottles in his hand. 'Okay, we've got a choice of an antiseptic cream or iodine.'

'Iodine.'

'You think?'

Nina shrugged. 'We might need the antiseptic cream elsewhere,' she said. 'Some of those scratches on his face and hands are quite deep.'

'True. Okay. Iodine it is.'

Nina poured the dark orange liquid onto a wad of gauze dressing, handed Ross the bottle, and leaned over the stranger.

As she applied the iodine to his bare skin, a curse escaped through Ross's lips, and he moved away from her.

'You're not helping,' she said through gritted teeth.

'Sorry.' He handed her the bottle and watched as she applied more of the liquid to the wound. 'He must be in a worse state than he looks if he didn't react to that.'

'Do you want to put some of that antiseptic cream on his face while I finish this?'

'Okay. We'll need to elevate his arm to stop the bleeding too. Put the other pillow under it.'

The sound of the radio playing music in between bursts of static at the front of the truck stop reached Nina's ears. For the past three hours, they'd heard the weather warnings increasing in urgency as the storm powered closer. After years of drought, it seemed the weather was finally going to bring some respite for the local farmers – if they and their crops could survive the incoming assault.

High winds and flash flooding had swept across much of the county, and a sense of foreboding permeated Nina's thoughts as she worked.

'Will your dogs be alright?' she asked, recapping the bottle of iodine.

Ross nodded. 'Tim would've put them in the barn for shelter,' he said. 'We haven't seen one of them for a week. God knows where she's gone.'

Nina noted his troubled tone. 'Does she usually wander off?'

'Yes. Misty's only three and treats the property like it's her own. She usually comes back after a couple of days, though, when she realizes how bad she is at hunting.'

'Hopefully someone will give her shelter.'

'Or she'll have already run home at the start of this.'

They finished their task in silence, each lost in their own thoughts.

Nina grabbed more gauze from the first aid kit, packed it against the wound, and then wrapped a bandage round the man's arm.

Her gaze fell to the stranger's face as Ross applied the last of the antiseptic cream, and she wondered if the man had been involved in some sort of car accident – the area was too remote to walk from place to place – and who did that anyway?

But a car accident didn't explain the wound to his shoulder, or the dirt that had covered his fingernails.

She sighed, frustrated, and began to bundle up the dirty linen before dropping it into a plastic bag and leaving it on the floor out of the way. She tore the gloves from her fingers and placed a new towel under the man's shoulder.

'Nina?'

'What's wrong?'

'I don't think we should mention Phil's theory about this being a knife wound to the others, do you?'

'I wish we could find out who he is,' she said. 'There must be someone worried about him.'

'Never mind who he is, Nina,' said Ross. 'More to the point – who did this to him?'

FOUR

Ross tore off his gloves, threw them in the trash can, and closed his eyes, desperate for a few seconds where he could avoid Nina's gaze.

He ran his hand over his face.

The fact that a complete stranger had turned up at the truck stop with a knife wound could only mean that something had gone very, very wrong with John's operation. And the only reason going around in circles in Ross's mind at that moment was that John's cover had been blown.

Wide open.

He'd had no idea they were going to make a move today, of all days – not with the storm's approach. His thoughts were jumbled, veering between wanting to jump in his truck to make sure his father and brother were out of danger, and wanting to stay put.

His heart beat painfully as he forced himself not to panic. Not until he could work out a way to ensure Nina was safe.

'Ross?'

He exhaled, opened his eyes, and massaged his temples. 'Sorry, what?'

'I said, do you think we should take turns looking after him?' A worried frown creased Nina's brow, and he realized he'd do anything to keep her safe.

He glanced at the man who lay passed out on the bed, then back to her, and nodded. 'Good idea. I don't think he's going anywhere, so I'll stay with him for a bit. If he doesn't wake up we can probably take turns checking on him every fifteen minutes or so.'

He watched as Nina finished tidying up the litter strewn around the room from their hasty rudimentary first aid and then stepped towards her.

'Nina, I can do that – go and sit down. We've both had a shock, and you've been working flat out since this morning.'

She opened her mouth to speak, and he silenced her by holding up his hand. 'Go – before I change my mind,' he said.

She nodded mutely, handed him the dressings she'd collected, and left the room.

He pulled the chair closer to the bed and eased into it. Paranoia began to peck at his nerves, and he rubbed his palms down his jeans, then sat back and pinched the bridge of his nose.

If John had been compromised, then were his father and Tim safe? Were they wondering what had happened to him?

Then there were Sean and Dani – two more strangers who had blown in with the storm. Where did they fit in? Were they really the innocent travelers they said they were, or was there something more sinister in their sudden appearance?

He looked up as a vicious gust of wind shook the exposed panes of glass and made a mental note to check the rest of the building for leaks.

A light snoring began to emanate from the wounded man beside him, and Ross eased away from the bed and finished tidying away the first aid kit.

As he worked, he forced his doubts from his mind, resolving to keep up appearances for Nina's sake and for their other unexpected guests.

Until he could be sure of what was going on in Mistake Creek tonight, he had to remain calm.

He straightened, set his shoulders, and silently cursed the day he'd met Special Agent John Asher, wondering how the hell he was going to get through the night.

———

A loud crack of thunder shook the building as Nina walked back into the front room of the truck stop.

Phil, Sean, and Dani were talking in low voices when she entered, and they looked up as she pushed through the counter door to join them.

'How is he?' asked Phil.

Nina collapsed into a chair next to him and rubbed her eyes. 'Still unconscious, although Ross seems to think it's more from exhaustion and that wound on his arm, not a head injury.' She pursed her lips. 'We couldn't find any wounds under his hair, so that's something.'

The others murmured in agreement.

Nina leaned back and closed her eyes, listening to the rain thrashing against the roof and walls.

That afternoon, she'd thought her biggest problem was going to be whether the building held together during the storm. Now, she had three guests and a wounded man to worry about.

And no idea how he'd been hurt.

'Here.'

She opened her eyes to find Ross standing above her, holding out a mug, the strong coffee aroma firing her senses.

'Get that down you – you didn't get a chance to finish the last one.'

'Thanks.'

She watched as he ran a hand over his face, his eyes weary. His brown hair curled lazily over the neckline of his checked shirt, his jeans worn on the seat and back pockets. She noticed a hole forming in the thin material covering one butt cheek as he turned away and bit her lip as she felt her face color.

Regret welled up inside her as she wondered whether they could have salvaged their friendship if she'd stayed in Mistake Creek instead of running away all those years ago. She'd been too embarrassed to stay after what had happened. She wondered if they'd get an opportunity to talk properly before the truck stop was sold and she had to return to the city. If anything, she wanted a chance to rekindle their friendship, and the hours spent together preparing for the storm had gone some way to rebuild the bridge between them.

Ross leaned down, pulled out one of the stools from under the counter next to her, and sank onto it with a sigh.

The rain pelted across the exposed areas of the canted tin roof, reminding Nina of small stones striking the surface.

She raised her head at the sound of the rain rushing through the gutters, clattering down the pipes towards the water tanks.

'Your father's going to be pleased about this,' she said.

'As long as the crops don't get damaged,' he replied. 'But, yes, hopefully this will make the difference this year.'

Phil wandered over to the phone fixed to the wall and lifted the receiver to his ear. 'Still nothing.'

'Well, our guest is sleeping, so I think he'll survive,' said Ross.

Nina sighed. 'We'll have to keep an eye on him.' She raised her eyes to the ceiling as a gust of wind pushed against the structure. 'I don't think anyone's going to be coming to get him tonight. The emergency services will have their hands full as it is.'

Ross spun on his heel to face Sean and Dani. 'You didn't see him when you were coming back from the creek?'

'No,' said Dani, shaking her head. 'We didn't see anyone.'

She checked over her shoulder, and Sean nodded.

'She's right – it's what got us thinking we were the only ones stupid enough to be out in this weather. That's why we turned back.'

Nina blew across the surface of her coffee. 'Given the state of him, I'm wondering if he walked cross-country,' she said, and took a sip.

'But where would he have come from?' Ross frowned. 'You didn't see anyone else at Hudson's, did you?'

'No, it was pretty quiet up there,' said Sean. 'We were the only ones – and Hudson didn't seem too pleased to see us.'

'Do you think he's going to be alright?' asked Dani. 'He seemed in a bad way.'

'Whatever caused the wound didn't go too deep,' said Nina. 'If we can make sure he rests and we keep it clean, I think he'll be okay until the emergency services can come and get him.' She took another sip of the coffee, relishing its warmth, and frowned. 'Ross, what did you do with his shirt?'

'What do you mean?'

'When we cut it off him. Where did you put it?'

'I think I just threw it on the floor with the dirty towels. Why?'

'Back in a minute.'

Nina hurried through the building to her bedroom.

Ross had left the door open in case the man had called out, but for the moment, the stranger was silent, his eyes closed and a slight frown creasing his brow.

Nina watched as his hands twitched in his sleep, as if he was trying to grasp something out of his reach, and she wondered what memories filled his dreams.

Or nightmares.

She walked over to where the man's jacket lay strewn across the back of a chair, discarded when she and Ross had begun to clean the wound. Picking up the jacket, she put her hand in the pockets, her fingers seeking out a driving licence, cell phone – anything that would give them a clue to his identity or what he was doing in Mistake Creek.

She bent down to the pile of bloodstained towels Ross had dropped on the floor and carefully rummaged through them using her fingertips until she found the fragments of his shirt they'd cut away. She gathered them up with the remnants of the jacket they'd torn from the stranger's body, checked the man was still sleeping, and made her way back to the front of the building.

'Here,' she said as she put the shirt on the counter. 'In all the panic, we forgot to check his pockets.'

Phil leaned across and pulled the main part of the shirt to one side and opened up the breast pockets. Nina watched as his fingers worked their way inside one, then the other, before she leaned over and took the smaller fragments. She traced her fingers around the cuff and seams, but nothing fell out. No labels, no pieces of paper, nothing.

'Well, that was a waste of time,' she said, disgusted, and threw the strips of fabric back.

'I wouldn't say that,' said Phil, and held up a small plastic bag.

Nina's eyes opened wide when she realized what was inside.

White powder.

FIVE

The room fell silent as everyone stared at the bag Phil held up between his fingers, before they all began talking at once.

Nina stared at the bag, letting the voices wash over her.

Drugs. In her father's truck stop. Found on a man who had, in all likelihood, been stabbed. And was now lying unconscious on her bed.

She turned and looked at the useless phone on the wall, then reached across to her handbag and pulled out her cell phone.

No signal.

Frustrated, she propped it on top of the landline telephone fixed to the wall and focused her attention back to the room as Sean's voice cut through the rest.

'I knew we shouldn't have stopped. Goddammit, I

shouldn't have listened to you,' he said, rounding on the woman with him. 'We should've kept going.'

'Hey!' said Nina, holding up her hand. 'All of you, quiet, *please*.'

A silence descended on the room.

She watched their faces. Even Ross seemed surprised at the strength in her voice.

'Thank you,' she said. 'Shouting over each other isn't going to help. And you stand a good chance of waking up our patient.'

She sighed and plucked the bag from Phil's grip. 'Are you even sure this is what you think it is?' She waved it at the four people who were staring at her. 'Well, are you?'

'What else could it be?' said Ross.

She glared at him. 'I don't know. I just think we're all jumping to conclusions here.'

'What do you suggest we do?' asked Dani.

'Maybe you should try it?' said Sean, turning to Ross, who frowned.

'Why me? How the hell should I know what drugs are like?'

'Don't tell me you never tried drugs at college?' said Nina.

He glared at her, before his face softened. 'Maybe, just once,' he said, looking sheepish. He held up his hand to silence the sudden chiming of voices. 'Give it to me,' he mumbled. 'I'll take a sniff.'

He snatched the bag back from Nina, and then unsealed the top of it, his dark eyes burning into hers.

She held her breath while he raised it to his nose and carefully sniffed at its contents.

'Nothing.'

A collective sigh escaped from the small group.

He resealed the bag and passed it to Nina.

She frowned and pointed at his hand. 'You've got some on your finger.'

Ross stared at his hand and then raised his finger to his mouth.

'No!' Phil rushed at him, knocking his hand down. 'Don't.'

Ross looked at him, a puzzled expression on his face.

Phil glanced to the others, then back at Ross. 'It's not like the movies. You're not going to be able to tell what it is just by tasting it,' he explained. 'And you don't even know if it *is* drugs. It could be rat poison or something.'

Ross stared at the powder on his finger and then rubbed it onto his jeans before pointing at the bag in Nina's hand. 'Go and put that in the safe in the office,' he said. 'Best place for it until we either work out who the hell that man is back there or the police show up.'

'Right.'

———

Nina pulled open the cupboard door, knelt, and pushed old files and piles of paperwork out of her way. She added sorting through the documents to her list of things to do, *if* things ever returned to normal after the storm passed, and stacked everything onto the floor beside her.

The combination safe had been set into the floor of the cupboard, and she'd only opened it once since arriving. She flicked the dial left and right and wrenched the door back.

In her haste, she knocked a photo and a ring box to the floor, and she grabbed them.

Slipping the bag of white powder into the safe, she turned the photograph over in her hand, her fingers easing the creases from the corners.

'What the hell would you make of this, Greg?' she murmured. She placed the photograph towards the back of the safe and slipped the ring box open. Three months after he'd died, she'd taken the engagement ring and wedding band off her left hand and had sealed them away in the box.

The car crash had been awful, yet the marriage had already been over for a year, and she struggled to be a grieving widow. They'd simply married too young, Nina looking for an excuse to try and forget her old life in Mistake Creek and the heartbreak she'd left behind. She'd put all her energy into her work in the years since, until the issues with her father's health had coincided with the loss of her job four weeks ago, and she'd had to return.

Resentment washed over her, closely followed by guilt.

She snapped the box shut and tucked it next to the photograph, then slammed the door shut.

'Nina?'

She looked up to see Ross leaning against the doorframe.

'Everything okay?'

'Sure,' she sniffled, then stood. Ross had never met her husband, and she wasn't going to start explaining everything to him now, not with four strangers in the building. 'How's everyone out there?'

'Nervous. The wind's getting up. I wouldn't mind seeing how those tarpaulins are holding up.'

Nina shook her head. 'Bad idea. There'll be all sorts of rubbish flying around out there.'

He shrugged. 'True. I'm just not very good at sitting around, doing nothing.'

'You never were.'

'Listen, Nina, I know how hard the past couple of days have been for you, coming back here, but I wanted to tell you. I think you're doing the right thing for your dad.'

She managed a smile. 'I haven't thanked you yet for keeping an eye on him until I could get him over to my place.' She ran her fingers through her ponytail. 'Thank goodness my neighbour there is looking after him.'

'It's the least I could do – especially after all these years.' He shoved his hands in the back pockets of his jeans. 'I just can't believe how fast his health has gone downhill. I mean, six weeks ago, he was fine.'

'The doctor I spoke to said that sometimes it happens that way – or he's been in denial about it and has managed to disguise his symptoms until recently.'

Ross visibly shivered. 'I'd hate to think what would've happened if I hadn't found him that day.' He pushed away from the doorframe. 'What do you think of our guests?' he asked, moving towards the scarred pine wood desk and running his hand across the dusty surface.

'I think they're one coffee away from a domestic argument,' said Nina, standing up and stretching.

'They're an odd couple, aren't they?'

'It takes all sorts.'

Nina pulled out the chair from under the desk and sank into it while Ross leaned against the desk, his hands gripping the edge. He appeared to be lost in thought.

'How are you holding up?' she asked. 'Are you worrying about your father and Tim?'

He shot a glance at her. 'No, they'll be fine.'

'Then what is it? You're all tensed up.'

He shrugged. 'I guess I'm wondering who the injured man is. I just hope he wakes up soon so we can ask him.'

'You never did like mysteries.'

He chuckled, relaxing a little. 'True. I like routine and order.' He smiled at her. 'Although you'd probably say that was boring.'

'Oh, I don't know – I think I could handle boring for a

while after tonight's excitement.' She covered her mouth with her hand and stifled a yawn.

'Nina? Why did you leave Mistake Creek without saying goodbye?'

The question caught her off guard; yet it had been hanging between them, unsaid, ever since she'd come back.

She sighed and leaned forward, her elbows on her knees. She stared at the whorls in the faded pattern of the worn carpet.

Whatever she said next, she didn't want to hurt Ross, but he was right. She owed him an explanation. She took a deep breath.

'I panicked,' she said. 'After what happened... I was so embarrassed...'

'So, you left? Without talking to me first?'

Nina leaned back in her seat and forced herself to look at him.

Anguish etched his face as he jutted his chin at the sealed door of the safe. 'So, what was he – an excuse to forget me?'

Nina reeled at the bitterness in his voice. She stood and paced towards the door. 'I should get back to our guests.'

'Wait – Nina, wait. I'm sorry.' Ross cleared the room in two strides and blocked the doorway with his arm. 'I'm sorry – I shouldn't have said that.'

Nina pursed her lips. 'No. You're right, Ross. You shouldn't.'

'I...'

A loud crash from the front of the truck stop was followed by a scream from Dani and shouting from the two men.

'Now what?' said Nina, her heart racing.

A split second later, the lights went out.

SIX

'What happened?'

Nina slid to a halt at the front counter, a flashlight in her hand, its wavering beam taking in the smashed window and glass covering the floor.

Rain breached the jagged opening, and a length of wood protruded through the broken panes of glass, swinging on a length of chain.

Beyond the broken glass, a shower of sparks fell from the sky onto the forecourt outside, a loud *hiss* carrying over the noise of the rain.

'The power line to the building's down,' said Sean. 'I think the wires have caught on something.'

'It's the signage,' said Ross. 'Looks like the wind dragged it from the roof.'

Nina hurried towards the counter and grabbed a broom, the wind whipping her hair around her face.

'Out of the way,' she called. 'Let's get this glass cleared up so we can plug the window with something.'

'Here,' said Phil, taking the broom from her. 'I'll do that.'

'Can we nail something up on the inside?' asked Sean. 'Do you have any spare boards?'

'Outside the back door,' said Ross.

The two men disappeared from view, and Nina began to sweep the broken glass to one side. As she finished, the men returned, carrying panels of plywood between them.

Nina stepped out of their way as Ross pushed the sign back out through the window, grabbed the nail-gun, and secured the boards, the noise from outside diminishing as soon as he'd finished.

'Okay,' she said, sweeping her hair out of her face. 'What about that power line?'

Ross hurried to the door and coaxed it open. His jaw clenched; then he slammed the door shut and locked it.

'Looks like it's blown at the mains or something,' he said. 'The sparks have stopped, but it could still be live.'

'Okay, well, as soon as it's light, we'll have to find something to keep people away from it,' said Nina. She looked at the growing piles of glass on the floor. 'I'll be back in a minute; I'll go and find something to put that in.'

She hurried back towards the small laundry, her heart hammering.

She'd been frightened when she'd heard the glass shatter and the lights went out, but now that she had something to do and could keep herself busy for a few minutes, she was able to fight down the urge to panic.

She felt a familiar tightness in her chest and leaned against the washing machine, placing the flashlight on the surface next to her and concentrating on her breathing.

At the sound of footsteps in the passageway, she began to search through the cupboards until she found the dustpan.

The beam from a second flashlight hit the wall beside her.

'Have you got any old newspapers?' asked Ross, appearing in the doorway. 'We should probably wrap those bigger pieces of glass.'

'Try looking in that cupboard there. I'll go make a start with this.'

She wandered back towards the sound of Phil sweeping the broom through the fallen glass at the front of the truck stop.

Sean was speaking, his tone urgent.

'We should've just kept going,' he said. 'We didn't need to stop. We should've just kept looking, dealt with the problem, and gotten the hell out of here.'

Nina paused before walking into the shop area, the low murmur reaching her ears, and switched off her flashlight. She flattened herself against the wall and held her breath.

'It's too late now,' said Dani. 'We'll stay here, see how things turn out. We can't go back to Hudson's place anyway.'

'It makes things complicated.'

Nina jerked her head away from the doorframe at the sound of a chair scraping the floor, switched on the flashlight, cleared her throat, and walked through the door.

'How are you both doing?'

Dani jumped at her entrance, a look of concern quickly replaced with a smile. 'Getting over the shock of your front window imploding,' she said, her tone light.

Nina's gaze flickered to Sean who had his back to her, adjusting the candles placed around the counter to shed more light around the room. He seemed distracted, disturbed by her sudden appearance.

'Me too.' Nina moved across the room to where Phil had swept the glass into piles and began gathering it up in the dustpan.

Ross joined her, a pile of newspapers under his arm while he dragged the large waste bin from the kitchen. He crouched beside her and began wrapping the glass.

'Having enough excitement yet?'

'I could do with a little less now, I think.'

They worked until most of the glass had been removed; then Ross took the dustpan from her.

'Me and Phil will finish here,' he said. 'Go and sit with our patient and grab some rest yourself.'

Nina rubbed her eyes. 'If you're sure?'

'Go on – go. I'll bring you a hot drink in a bit.'

———

Nina looked up from her book as the wounded man moaned and tried to roll over onto his side.

The movement tugged the covers down to his waist and tangled them around his legs as he thrashed out in his agitated state.

Nina folded the page down, dropped the book onto the chair, and moved next to him.

She gently rolled him back. 'You need to stay still,' she said. 'You've been injured, and you've got a bad cut on that side as well.'

His eyes flickered open, then closed again, a low groan escaping his lips.

'Where am I?' he whispered.

'Mistake Creek Truck Stop,' she said. 'We think you've been stabbed, but you're safe now.'

His eyelids flickered again, and a frown puckered his brow before he twisted his head away. His chest began to rise and fall as he drifted back to sleep.

Nina rearranged the pillow under his head and pulled the blanket up, wondering again how he'd ended up on her doorstep.

Not a local. Ross's words echoed in her head.

So, none of them knew who the mysterious stranger was, where he came from, or whether he would harm them.

Her fingers traced the curve of his shoulder as she checked the bandage wrapped around it. A little blood covered the centre, and she frowned. The last thing they needed was an infection to take hold before they could get medical help for him.

He began to snore softly, and Nina sighed, realising that she'd be none the wiser until either he regained consciousness or medical help reached them. And that wouldn't happen until the creek level had subsided or the landslide had been cleared – whichever came sooner.

Somehow, she didn't think he'd be able to afford the costs of a medivac if the emergency services deemed a helicopter extraction necessary.

Nina picked up her book and slumped back into the chair next to the bed, trying to concentrate on the words as she flicked the pages.

She jumped at a sound from the passageway, then relaxed as Ross appeared carrying a steaming mug of coffee.

'Here,' he murmured, handing the drink to her. 'I thought you could do with this.'

'Thanks.'

'How's he doing?' he asked. 'I thought I heard voices?'

Nina shrugged and blew across the hot surface of the drink. Something in the tone of Ross's voice made her hesitate before she answered.

'It was nothing. He was mumbling. Incoherent.'

'Huh.' Ross looked over his shoulder at the figure on the bed. 'Hopefully he won't get an infection.'

'That's what I'm afraid of.'

She managed a smile as he reached down and rubbed her arm.

'We've done everything we can for him, Nina. With any luck, we'll be able to get through on the phone in the morning and call for help.'

'I know. I just feel responsible for him until then.'

'You always were the one who insisted on caring for the injured wildlife we found as kids.'

Nina laughed. 'Yeah, some things don't change, do they?'

He grinned and pointed at the coffee cup in her hands. 'Drink that. Give me a call if you want more or need a break, and I'll take over.'

'Thanks.'

She lowered her gaze back to her book as Ross turned and left the room, and she tried to concentrate on the words in front of her. Several minutes passed before she looked across to the stranger lying on the bed.

She wondered if anyone was looking for him, whether someone, somewhere, was worried that he hadn't returned home.

Or whether he had a home.

She tossed the book aside after she caught herself reading the same paragraph for the third time.

A gust of wind shook the building, and she raised her eyes to the windowpanes, which still rattled as if the wind was trying to tear them from the framework.

Another thought struck her, and she stepped back to

the narrow bed and gently picked up his left hand. No tell-tale marks of a wedding band were visible against his tanned skin.

She moved his hand, running her fingers over his skin. Rough, a few cuts – not deep – and not the hands of an office worker. An outdoors type then, but doing what?

Nina exhaled loudly, frustrated. She hated mysteries too. Everything in her life up until the storm was ordered, precise. Controlled.

Then the man's fingers tightened round her own, and she gasped as he pulled her down towards him.

'Don't make a sound, Nina. Your life depends on me.'

SEVEN

'What the hell?'

The man slowly let Nina's fingers slip through his, watching her intently.

Her mind reeled. 'What's going on?' She glanced over her shoulder, towards the open door. Ross was only seconds away. All she had to do was scream, and he'd be there.

'Don't scream,' murmured the injured man. 'I won't hurt you, okay?'

She looked down to where he lay, her heart racing.

His gaze held hers. 'Whatever you do, keep your voice down.'

She took a step back, startled. 'What do you mean?'

'You're in danger, Nina. I have to get you away from here,' he said, his face calm. 'I'm telling the truth. Please believe me,' he whispered. 'You can't trust anyone.'

His eyes were alert, any sign of fever gone – if he'd had a fever.

The confused man who had asked where he was only a short time ago had disappeared. In his place lay a man fully aware of his surroundings, his whispered voice belying a strength as yet unseen.

Nina sank into the chair next to the bed, her legs shaking. She placed her hands on her thighs and tried to ignore the thump of her heart.

'I'm sorry I scared you,' he said. 'I didn't mean to.'

Nina raised her hand. 'Shut up a minute, okay?'

She closed her eyes and breathed, forcing the air into her lungs, fighting down the panic.

'Are you okay?'

She opened her eyes and glared at him. 'I'm asthmatic. Unless you want me to pass out before you've had a chance to explain yourself, shut up and let me breathe.'

'Have you got an inhaler?'

Nina ignored him while she waited until her lungs filled with oxygen and the wheezing subsided. 'It's in the front room, on the counter.'

'You should carry it on you.'

She glared at him, and he fell silent again, watching her. She exhaled, then stood, waiting for any dizziness to wash over her. When it didn't, she stepped closer to the bed.

'I'm sorry.'

59

She raised her hand. 'You said. How do you know my name?'

'Lucky guess. I'm guessing this was your father's business?' He didn't wait for her response. 'We've had the place under surveillance for a while now. I didn't realize you were back.'

'What's going on?' She crossed her arms. 'Why am I in danger?'

'Keep your voice down. There are some bad people here,' he whispered. 'I recognized a man's voice.' He raised his gaze to the open door. 'Who's here – apart from you?'

'Why should I tell you?'

'Please.' His eyes bored into her. 'I promise I won't hurt you, but I need to know who else is here if I'm going to protect you.'

'I don't *need* protecting!' Nina hissed.

'Yes, you do. You just don't realize it yet.' He reached out for her hand. 'Please, tell me.'

She sighed. 'There's a truck driver, Phil, who's staying overnight because of the storm. Apparently he's a local, but I've only met him today for the first time. A man and a woman turned up on a motorbike about half an hour before you showed up – we've persuaded them to stay rather than push on towards town too. The road floods about six miles from here. Then there's Ross Flanagan– he's local. His father owns a farm; he's there now with Ross's younger brother. Ross has been helping me here and couldn't get away in time to beat the storm.'

He nodded and then frowned. 'What do the couple with the motorbike look like?'

'Dani's shorter than me, long blonde hair, about forty I guess. Sean is older. Short silver hair. Tall, broad across the shoulders.'

His grip tightened, and she noticed his jaw clench. 'How long have you known this Ross guy?'

'Why?'

'Humour me.'

'We were at school together. I only came back three days ago. My father's ill – I'm selling this place.' She stopped and put her hand to her brow. 'Why the hell am I telling you all of this?'

'You need to understand – you can trust me.'

'Who stabbed you?'

'It's better you don't know.'

'Did you fight back?'

'I didn't have time.'

'Where were you?'

'About four miles from here.'

'And you walked?'

'Nina, listen to me.' He grasped her hand tighter. 'You have to do what I tell you.'

'What?' She tried to pull away.

'*Listen* to me,' he urged. 'We're in a lot of trouble. I don't know if –'

They both fell silent at the sound of footsteps.

The stranger squeezed Nina's hand and then let go.

'Cover for me,' he said, and closed his eyes. 'Please trust me.'

Nina twisted round as Ross appeared in the doorway, a perplexed look on his face.

'Everything okay here? I thought I heard voices.'

Nina glanced at the stranger, his eyes closed, jaw slack, and then back to Ross.

'Yes. He was mumbling in his sleep. I couldn't make out a word he said.'

'Poor bastard.' Ross joined her and slipped an arm round her shoulders. 'How are you holding up?'

'Tired, I guess. A bit stressed out.'

'Your breathing's a bit rough. Where's your inhaler?'

'In my bag.'

He squeezed her closer. 'Best go and get it. Last thing you need is to lose that.'

The sound of a polite cough interrupted them. Ross's arm dropped from her shoulders.

Phil stood in the doorway. 'Got a minute?' he asked, and beckoned them away from the room.

They followed him into the passageway.

'What's up?' said Ross.

'Listen, I was just thinking,' said Phil. 'The rain's eased a bit – why don't I drive up the road and see how things look?' He jutted his chin towards the room. 'I don't know about you, but I'm worried about that wound of his.

The sooner he gets a doctor to take a look at him, the better.'

Nina peered over her shoulder at the man on the bed, who snored quietly, his good arm flung across the pillow as he slept. She thought she saw his eyelids twitch. 'It makes sense,' she said. 'But I don't think you should be taking your truck. What happens if you get stuck? You won't be able to turn it around.'

Ross nodded. 'She's right. But what about taking my pick-up truck? I'll go with you.'

'And leave her here with three strangers?'

Ross sighed. 'Fair point.' He looked at Nina. 'What do you think?'

'You could always take my dad's old pick-up truck,' she suggested to Phil. 'It's got a full tank of fuel, and the tires are in good condition.'

Phil grinned. 'Perfect. I'll need a flashlight as well. Maybe some rope, just in case?'

'There's plenty of rope in the back of it,' said Nina. 'And there's a spare flashlight on the counter in the front room – help yourself.' She pulled the car keys from her pocket and tossed them to Phil. 'Just make sure you bring it and yourself back in one piece, okay?'

'Yes, ma'am.'

EIGHT

Once Phil had disappeared through the back door and run towards the truck, Nina shut the door and followed Ross back through the building to the shop area at the front.

Sean was standing next to the front door, peering out through the glass panel, while Dani paced back and forth behind him. They both wheeled round at the sound of footsteps.

'What's going on?' said Dani. 'Where's he going?'

Candlelight flickered across her face, highlighting the frown lines that creased her brow.

Nina resisted the urge to ask why the other woman was so concerned about Phil's intentions, replaying the conversation with the wounded stranger in her mind. Instead, she turned to Ross, who held up his hand in an effort to calm the other woman.

'It's okay. Phil's going to take a look at the creek level, to see if the bridge has flooded or not.'

'We need to think about getting that man some medical help, if we can,' said Nina.

The headlight beam from the truck shone through the gaps in the wooden boards as the vehicle drove across the forecourt. Its brake lights flickered once before they heard the roar of its engine over the rain beating on the roof.

Sean returned his gaze to the gap in the door. 'How long do you think he'll be?'

Ross shrugged. 'Half an hour, maybe. Depends on how bad the road is.'

The other man grunted in reply.

Dani stalked across the room, flung herself onto one of the stools, and crossed her arms.

'I guess we just wait then,' she pouted.

———————

Kyle Roberts concentrated on keeping his breathing steady, despite the temptation to open his eyes, grab Nina and run, that encroached on his training and common sense.

When the older man had made the suggestion to see if he could make it into town, he knew his time was limited. Now, he was still stuck here, waiting and hoping he'd get a chance to do the right thing.

He twisted his head, the soft cotton pillowcase

feathering his cheek, the scent of Nina's perfume permeating his senses, and forced himself to concentrate.

Two men were still in the building – the neighbour, Ross, and a stranger who had appeared on a motorbike with a pillion passenger.

He listened to Ross's voice in the background. Could the farmer's son be trusted, or was he the one who had blown their cover?

Someone had.

He cursed under his breath. He'd expected the truck stop to be abandoned, considering the boards that were nailed over the windows. He hadn't factored the owner's daughter being there, or her preparations for the incoming storm, into his plans. John hadn't mentioned she'd returned after all this time.

Now he'd endangered her.

He shuffled under the covers she'd pulled up to his chin, the tightness of the bandages she'd wrapped around his arm and shoulder restricting movement.

It had hurt like hell when she and Ross had cut away his shirt and dressed the wound, the procedure taking all his stamina not to yell out when the iodine had been applied.

By the time they'd finished, he'd been genuinely exhausted, but relieved to know the knife had only pierced soft tissue and stood a good chance of healing well – if he could get out of the truck stop alive.

His thoughts returned to the couple on the motorcycle.

It couldn't be coincidence that they'd apparently appeared moments before he'd reached the truck stop.

His gut clenched, and he realized they must have been sent out to hunt him down. If they knew who he was, then Nina's life was at risk every minute he stayed with her.

The sooner he could reach a phone, the better for them both.

As he'd approached the truck stop, he'd seen the phone lines swinging in the wind, but they were still intact.

What he couldn't know until he tried was whether the lines held all the way to the exchange, or whether the storm had uprooted trees and damaged the precious connection.

He wondered if John had managed to escape.

He rubbed the palm of his hand over his face. He couldn't assume John had raised the alarm, which meant he still had to find a working phone, or another means to get help – and fast.

Kyle gritted his teeth, vowing revenge. He raised his head off the pillow, turning to take in the temporary dressing that covered the upper part of his arm. He'd been lucky.

He groaned, the room spinning, before he let his head fall back. He'd never known such tiredness.

Sure, he'd been stabbed before – shot once, too – but the accumulation of stress undercover for six months followed by the night's events had caught up with him.

Somehow, he had to find a way to fight the exhaustion and get to a working phone without alerting his enemies.

If they weren't already in the building with him.

———

Nina chewed a fingernail while she waited by the front door.

The boarded-up windows next to her stifled the room but did little to stop the sound of rain lashing the panes of glass.

Dani and Sean had set themselves up at one end of the counter, talking in muted tones. Nina let their voices wash over her, mulling over the strange conversation with the man sleeping in her bed, either passed out or doing a very good impression of a man who had passed out.

What the hell had he meant about her being in danger? And why all the questions about Ross and who else was in the building? She sighed, annoyed with herself. The stranger was delirious, delusional. He'd been injured, somehow, and had then walked through the storm for help. It was no wonder he was scared.

As Nina checked her watch again, Ross slipped beside her.

'Anything?'

'Not yet.' She craned her neck and peered out the small opening they'd left in the wood paneling to use as a peep-hole through the glass. 'It's been nearly an hour. That's

68

more than enough time to get as far as the creek and back, isn't it?'

'I'd have thought so.'

'Hmm.' She sighed. 'Did you phone your dad?'

'There's still no signal, and I can't get through on the landline either.' He shrugged. 'I'm sure they'll be fine. Dad's lived through a few of these storms over the years, and Tim was nearly finished boarding the house up when I drove down here.'

'Do you think Phil's okay?' said Nina. 'Should we go and find him?'

Ross frowned. 'Give it another ten minutes,' he said. He pushed her gently to one side and peered out through the opening in the boards. 'It's getting worse out there again, so he's probably being careful, driving slowly.'

'We should never have let him go.'

Ross snorted. 'He would've gone anyway – I've been watching him since the storm started. I don't think he liked being cooped up in here.'

'Do you think he'll go all the way into town?'

'I think he was just planning to check the creek level across the main road, that's all. If he can get into town, I'd expect him to come back here to get his truck first. Try not to worry too much.'

He pulled her into a hug and lowered his mouth to hers.

Nina turned her head and raised her hands. 'Ross, I –

I'm sorry. This isn't the time.' She sighed and rested her forehead on his chest. 'Sorry.'

He rested his chin on her head, and she felt his breath across her hair. 'No, Nina – I'm sorry. I couldn't help it.' He straightened. 'I'm glad you came back.'

'Ross, when this storm is over, we need to talk.' She sighed. 'I've got so much I need to say to you.'

'Same here. I've missed you, you know, and you looked so sad for a moment there.' He straightened and rubbed her arm. 'I'll always be here for you; you know that, right?'

She nodded and then squinted as a vehicle swept into the forecourt, its headlights momentarily blinding her as it passed the door and slid to a halt.

'He's back.'

Ross moved away from her and opened the door, then stood back to let Phil in.

A gust of wind blew the door out of his hand, sending it crashing against a shelving unit behind it. Rain blew through the opening, seeking a way into the building.

Nina cringed as a flash of lightning illuminated the sky above the canopy, followed a moment later by a crash of thunder that shook the walls with its ferocity.

A silhouetted figure dashed across the forecourt towards them, hunched against the rain and strong wind.

As Phil stumbled over the threshold, Ross slammed the door, a muted rumble of thunder echoing against it.

Nina took one look at the expression on Phil's face and rushed to his side.

Hands shaking, he let her help him out of his overcoat and then removed his hat, throwing it onto the counter. Water began to pool around his feet, but Nina ignored it, more concerned with his pale complexion.

'What's wrong?' she said, taking him by the arm. 'What happened? Are you okay?'

He shook his head and took the towel that Ross passed to him. After drying off the worst of the water, he leaned against the counter.

Sean and Dani had joined them, worry creasing their faces.

'What's going on?' asked Dani, clutching Sean's arm.

'Phil?' urged Ross. 'You're beginning to worry us. Did you manage to cross the creek?'

'No. No, I didn't.' Phil paused, took a deep breath, and rested his shaking hands on the counter.

'There's a dead man in a car parked near the creek. He's been shot.'

NINE

'Here, sit down,' said Nina, coaxing Phil onto one of the stools next to the counter. 'Your legs are shaking.'

She tried to ignore her own hands, which trembled as she spoke.

Phil allowed himself to be seated, then leaned an elbow on the counter and rubbed his hand over his face. 'Sorry – I'll be okay in a minute.'

Ross squeezed his shoulder. 'Take it easy. You've had one hell of a shock.' He turned to Nina. 'Do you want to grab that spare blanket from your bedroom? I think Phil might feel a bit better if we can get him dry and warm.'

'Sure.' Nina hurried out of the shop area and down the passageway towards her room. She slowed as she approached, peered round the door frame, and exhaled when she saw the stranger fast asleep, facing towards her, his arm draping over the side of the bed.

She ran her hand through her hair, her mind racing.

The man had sounded genuinely concerned for her safety earlier, so was he capable of killing another man?

What was the connection between him and the dead man Phil had discovered in the pick-up truck next to the swollen creek?

She cursed under her breath, realising that she should have demanded he tell her his name when he was awake and they were alone.

The stranger stirred in his sleep, snorted, then rolled away from her, his features hidden.

She moved quietly across the room, grabbed the spare blanket from the foot of the bed, and pulled a towel from the linen cupboard before she crept out again. She went to pull the door shut, frowned, and then pushed it open again.

Just in case.

Returning to the front of the building, she hurried to Phil's side.

Sean stood nearby, concern etched across his features. Dani clung to him, her face pale in the light from the candles on the counter next to her.

Ross took the blanket from Nina and wrapped it round the shivering man's shoulders.

'Here, dry your hair,' said Nina. 'I'll make you a hot drink in a minute.'

Phil nodded, toweled his hair, and then scrunched the material between his fingers, his breathing heavy.

73

'You said you saw a dead man?' prompted Sean. 'Where was he?'

Phil ran a hand through his damp hair. 'Just before the creek floods the road,' he said. 'It looks like his car lost control or something – it's over to one side of the asphalt, on the verge.' He swallowed. 'I only saw it because my headlights caught the reflectors on the back of the car. I thought he might have been stranded – you know, bogged down in the mud – and I was worried the creek might flood even worse than it has, so I stopped behind the car and went to see if I could help. I – sorry...'

He broke off, and Nina looked away as he tried to gather his wits.

'I'm sorry – I just keep seeing him,' he said, wiping his eyes.

Ross squeezed Phil's shoulder. 'You're doing fine,' he said. 'How do you know he'd been shot?'

'When I reached the driver's seat, I found him slumped over the steering wheel,' said Phil. 'I thought he was asleep, so I went to give him a shake to wake him up.' He hiccupped. 'Then I saw all the blood over the windshield and in his hair.' He stopped again, and a tear splashed his cheek. 'I've never seen a man shot in the head before.'

'Jesus,' murmured Ross. His eyes met Nina's.

She shook her head. She couldn't speak. Instead, she placed her hands on her hips and moved away from Phil and the others while she tried to hold herself together.

Sure, she knew that sort of thing happened in the larger

towns, and certainly in the cities with their problems of overcrowding, under-employment, and drug abuse, but *here*?

And why?

Who was the man? What had he done to deserve such a violent end?

She heard Ross, still asking questions, his voice a gentle murmur.

'Phil? What are the roads like?'

The other man sniffed. 'The creek's burst its banks. The water level's covered the bridge. The road was underwater for about four hundred yards leading up to the bridge. It looked like it was still rising.'

'No chance of getting the emergency services here tonight then.'

'I doubt it.'

'Nina?'

She looked up at Ross's voice. He'd moved closer to her, concern in his eyes.

'Are you going to be okay?'

She nodded. 'I think so.'

'Good.' He glanced over his shoulder at Phil as the man rubbed the towel between his fingers to coax the cold from his hands. 'Stay here. I'll be back in a minute.'

Nina jumped as Ross pushed past her and wrenched open the front door.

She followed him as far as the threshold and then squinted through the torrential rain as he sprinted over to his truck. She shrugged at Sean and Dani who were staring at her, frowns on their faces.

'I don't know what he's doing, either,' she said, and returned her gaze to the forecourt.

————

Ross hurried towards his truck, his feet sloshing through deep pools of water collecting in the pot-holed surface of the garage forecourt while rain dripped from his chin and nose.

His feet slid in the mud, and he threw out his arms for balance as he ran, the deafening torrent of rain obliterating any other sounds around him. By the time he reached the vehicle, his clothes were soaked through, the cold water leaching into his skin.

Climbing into the tray on the back of the truck, he staggered forward until he reached the locked aluminum toolbox mounted near the back of the cab. He knelt, ignoring the water that ran off his hat and down his neck, and reached into his pocket. Extracting a small bunch of keys, his fingers located the small one he sought, and he unlocked the toolbox.

Holding the metal lid open enough to reach inside, but keeping it at an angle so the contents would remain dry, he leaned forward, extending his arm until his fingers touched cold metal. He tightened his grip and pulled.

The next flash of lightning illuminated the barrel of the

hunting rifle, its firing mechanism and wooden stock wrapped in an old towel to protect them.

He swung the weapon over his arm and then reached back into the toolbox and pulled out a sports bag, looping its long canvas strap over his shoulder.

He let the lid fall shut, relocked the toolbox, and slid back to the ground.

Next, he wrenched open the driver's door. He clenched his teeth and swallowed hard as he remembered John's instructions.

If something goes wrong, do anything you can to slow them down.

He reached out and pulled the keys from the ignition, stuffed them into his pocket, then swung the cab door shut and stalked back to the building.

Nina's eyes opened wide as Ross pushed his way through the door, the rifle slung across his shoulder and the bag in his hand.

'Ross, what are you doing?'

He slung the bag on the counter, loaded the rifle, and swung himself onto a stool, the weapon balanced across his knee.

'I'm not taking any chances. Either there's a killer out there in that storm, or,' he said, his jaw set, 'he's lying on his back in your bed with a stab wound to his shoulder.'

TEN

Lightning split the clouds overhead, an electrifying crackle that shook the walls of the building.

'That was close,' said Ross, and Nina heard the slight tremor in his voice before he handed the rifle to her and disappeared to the back of the building.

Nina leaned over and pushed the buttons on the front of the radio, trying to pick up something other than static.

A faint mist of voices and music faded in and then out again before being lost to the airwaves.

She gave up and turned the volume down, the hiss of white noise beginning to grate on her nerves.

She resisted the urge to try the telephone again. With the storm so close, it was unlikely it'd be working, and she had no intention of receiving an electric shock if the line was hit at the same time the receiver was in her hand.

It would have to wait.

She stared up at the ceiling. Above their heads, the tin roof creaked as it tried to break free from the joists. Somewhere, a corner flapped in the wind, and she crossed her fingers, hoping the wind would change direction before the panel was ripped from the structure.

Rain lashed the windows in waves, buffeted by the wind. At one point, she thought the windows would crack under the pressure, the droplets pummeling the panes of glass.

She spun at the sound of footsteps on the tiled floor and raised her eyebrows as Ross joined her, a bottle in his hand.

'Bourbon?'

He shrugged, put five glasses on the counter, and uncapped the bottle. 'I spent enough time here with your father to know where he keeps the emergency supplies,' he said, tipping a generous quantity of the amber liquid into each of the glasses.

Nina frowned, wondering if there was more to his off-hand remark, whether he was chiding her for being gone so long. She shuffled on the stool, thinking of her father and Ross becoming so close in her absence that they regularly shared a drink.

She watched as he slid one of the drinks along the counter to Phil who stopped it, then held up the glass in a toast to Ross. 'Just what the doctor ordered,' he said, his hand shaking.

Ross nodded and handed glasses to Sean and Dani. 'Here. We've all had a shock. This might help.'

Handing back the rifle, Nina accepted her drink from Ross and savoured the warm burn as the liquid hit the back of her throat. She closed her eyes, trying to block out the thought of Ross sitting with her father here in the evenings, when she'd been hundreds of miles away in the city, trying to put as much space between herself and Mistake Creek as she could.

When she opened her eyes, he was staring at her over the top of his drink.

Then he turned away, and the moment passed.

She noticed that Sean held his glass in his hand, not drinking, but Dani had already finished hers and had placed her glass on the floor next to her feet.

'Why are you selling the business?' she asked, and stretched, cat-like, before curling her feet up under her.

'My father's been running the business for years,' said Nina, grateful for the excuse to take her mind off the evening's events for a brief moment. 'He used to do well with the accommodation block out the back, but the drought scared the tourists away – no-one's interested in seeing the valley struggling.' She shrugged. 'I've got no idea how Ross's neighbour is doing so well – everyone else around here is desperate, but he seems to be doing okay.'

'That's the Hudson place we stopped at, right?' said Dani.

Nina nodded. 'I don't know him personally – there was a different owner of that farm when I used to live here.'

'He's probably got other businesses elsewhere that help to prop it up,' said Phil. He shrugged. 'That's what I've heard anyway. And he's not exactly legitimate,' he added.

'Really?' Nina twisted in her chair to face him. 'What do you mean?'

In response, he pointed to the fragments of the stranger's shirt strewn across the counter.

'That white powder? I reckon that's something to do with him.'

'What makes you so sure?'

'I hear things, when I'm driving around here. It wouldn't surprise me at all if he was involved.'

Nina lowered her gaze and wondered if the liquor was starting to have an effect on Phil's imagination.

Phil pushed his stool away from the counter and wandered across to where Ross sat. He reached out for the half-empty bottle and held it up.

'Can I?'

Ross nodded.

'Thanks.'

Phil picked up the bottle, pushed through the counter door, and began walking towards the back of the building.

'Where are you going?' called Nina.

He held up the bottle, and jerked his head towards the

bedroom. 'I'm going to go back and keep an eye on our guest,' he said, and disappeared from sight.

Nina stood to follow him.

'Let him go,' murmured Ross.

'Are you sure?'

He nodded. 'He's had a shock. It's probably better to let him get drunk after what he's been through.'

She placed her own half-finished drink on the counter and moved to the front door, peering out at the intermittent flashes of lightning that illuminated the road and the fields beyond.

She thought of all the years of drought that had held the valley in its clutches for so long, and the relief the farmers would be feeling as they lay in their beds, the sound of rain pelting tin roofs and gutters.

Ross joined her, ducked his head to see through the exposed glass, and slipped an arm around her shoulders.

'How's it looking out there?'

'Nasty,' she murmured, leaning into him. 'I'm so glad those people had the sense to come here.'

'Yeah, I wouldn't want to be riding a motorbike in this weather,' he said. He glanced over his shoulder, then back to her. 'Listen, if you need to get some rest, I don't mind playing host for a couple of hours. You've had a long day.'

'Thanks.' She shivered. 'I'm okay at the moment. I'm more concerned with the roof, to be honest.'

'I know. You look up to the ceiling every time there's a gust of wind.'

'This is the last thing I needed, Ross.' She groaned. 'No offence, but I thought I'd be heading back tomorrow once I'd got a few things sorted out and some photographs taken for the real estate agency.'

He leaned against the wall and shoved his hands in his pockets. 'None taken. I realized this afternoon when we were working outside that you might not come back for good.' He shrugged. 'I wish you'd think about staying though.'

He looked so dejected that Nina reached out and squeezed his arm.

'If I do go back, I'll still visit.'

'What? Like you have over the past ten years?'

Nina let her hand fall away. 'I didn't mean to leave it so long,' she said. 'I've been so busy.'

Even to her ears, it sounded a flimsy excuse.

Ross eased himself off the wall and looked down at her. 'Do me a favour, Nina?'

'What?'

'Don't make promises you've got no intention of keeping. Not to me.'

He hurried to the counter and began rifling through the sports bag he'd brought in from his truck, and then swung the bag over his shoulder.

'I'm going to store this out of the way in your bedroom, if that's okay?'

Nina ignored the hint of sarcasm in his voice and nodded. 'Sure.'

Dani glanced up as Ross stalked past her, an exasperated look on her face, and lowered the cell phone in her hand.

'Still no signal,' she said. She dropped the phone back into her bag, before changing the subject. 'So, where does the name "Mistake Creek" come from?'

'The early settlers thought they'd find water here, but they were a few miles off course, hence "Mistake Creek",' said Nina. 'The actual creek is further up the road – the one that's flooded.'

'I can't believe we were so close to town before we had to turn back,' said Dani.

'Hopefully by the time you've had a night's sleep, the worst of this will be over.'

Dani snorted. 'I don't think I'll be sleeping with *that* noise above my head.' She raised her finger.

'I always found that relaxing,' said Nina as the rain beat on the tin roof. 'I guess it's because I grew up with it.'

'You grew up here?' The woman's voice was incredulous. 'In a truck stop?'

Nina grinned. 'Sure did. I caught the bus to school every day from over the road there.' She pointed beyond the boarded-up windows, and then her face fell. 'Seems like a lifetime ago.'

She pointed towards the passageway. 'We lived back there. Two bedrooms, a kitchen, and a bathroom,' she said. 'Just before I left to go to college, my dad added the accommodation block round the back. He did really well for a while.'

The other woman arched an eyebrow. 'This story doesn't sound like it has a happy ending.'

Nina shrugged. 'The business has been struggling because of the drought. There aren't as many tourists passing through as there used to be, and then my father moved back to the city with me last week,' she said. 'Although I've had my suspicions for the past month about his health problems, it took a while for him to listen to reason, despite some compelling evidence.'

Dani gestured at the bare walls. 'So, what are you going to do with the place?'

'Sell it,' said Nina, without hesitation. She bit her lip, realising how abrupt she'd sounded. 'I–I can't run the place. I came back to get the place ready for the real estate agent, that's all.'

She returned to her seat and rested against the counter, nibbled the side of her nail, and then looked at her finger, realising she'd bitten the nail to the quick.

Ross's reaction had left her confused. One moment, he seemed keen to explore a possible future with her; the next he was fuming because she was selling the truck stop.

She swore under her breath. She hated being cooped up at the best of times, let alone with four strangers and a man who was still sulking about her life choices.

Until she was nineteen, everyone in the area knew her business. When her wish for a relationship with Ross had been unfulfilled, she'd felt restricted by her surroundings and judged by him and their friends.

Leaving seemed the only option at the time, and she still maintained it had been for the best. Then why, now, the slight tinge of regret to her memories and the fact that she hadn't tried to at least maintain their friendship?

Nina stirred as Ross returned to the room, a slight color to his cheeks.

She wondered whether he was angry or embarrassed by the earlier episode.

Maybe he was as confused about the whole situation as she had been.

She groaned and rubbed her eyes.

Maybe Ross was right. Maybe she should get some sleep and see what the morning brought.

She raised her head from her hands at an exasperated sigh from Dani.

The woman had unfurled her legs and was standing, stretching her hands over her head, exposing her waist and a black tattoo that stretched from the waistband of her jeans up her ribcage. She exhaled again, loudly, and then turned to Sean.

'You were right. We should never have stopped here.'

'What?' He frowned. 'You're joking, right? You're changing your mind now?'

Dani put her hands on her hips. 'This is crazy. There's a man out the back there with a stab wound; there's a dead man in a car up the road – what sort of place *is* this?'

She wheeled round to face Nina, an accusing expression covering her features. 'I'll bet we could've crossed the creek if we'd just kept going like you said, Sean. I should've listened to you, not *her*.'

'Hey.' Nina raised her hands up. 'It's not my fault you're stuck here,' she said. 'And you're lucky you are.'

'Lucky?' Dani's eyebrows shot upwards. 'Are you kidding?'

'Oh, stop it,' said Nina, exasperated. She pushed herself up from the chair and stalked towards the front door. 'All the windows are boarded up,' she said over her shoulder. 'The back door is secure. And now,' she said, reaching up and sliding the bolt across the top of the front door, 'so is this one.'

She folded her arms. 'No-one's going to get in now without us knowing about it.' She glared at Sean who was frowning at her over the top of his wife's head. 'Or out.'

ELEVEN

'I wonder who the dead man is?' Nina pulled at the skin next to her thumbnail, distracted for a moment, then looked up at Ross. 'Any ideas?'

He frowned, leaned against the counter top, and folded his arms. 'No. I should've asked Phil about the vehicle, seen if he recognized it from town or something.'

He flexed his fingers, cracking his knuckles, before folding his hands behind his head and stretching.

'You don't think Phil hurt the man out by the creek, do you?' asked Nina, needing something to think about other than the tanned flesh showing under Ross's t-shirt. 'I mean, I've only met him today. He's telling the truth, isn't he?'

Ross leaned forward and rubbed his hands on his knees before he spoke. 'I don't think he hurt him,' he said. He peered over Nina's head towards the sofa where Dani and

Sean sat, then lowered his voice. 'I've known him for a while. He's always seemed honest. Whenever I've been here with your father and Phil's stopped for gas, he's always taken the time to stop and talk.' He shrugged. 'I've never taken him for the sort of person who has secrets.'

'Excuse me?'

Nina and Ross turned as one at the sound of the voice.

Sean stood at the end of the counter. 'Sorry to interrupt,' he said, 'but can I use the men's room?'

'Of course,' said Nina. 'It's down the passageway – third door on the left.'

'Thanks.'

'Here.' Ross walked over to the collection of emergency supplies. 'You'll need this,' he said, passing him a flashlight.

'True.' Sean grinned and took the flashlight before disappearing down the passageway and out of sight.

Nina rubbed her hand over her eyes, stifling a yawn.

'You okay?' Ross leaned over and squeezed her shoulder, his earlier outburst unspoken between them.

'Yeah. Just a bit tired.'

'Well, it's been a strange day.'

Nina leaned her elbows on the counter and rested her chin in her palms. 'What do you think is going on, Ross?'

'I have no idea.' He leaned away from her on the stool and looked across at Dani, who was flicking through an old issue of a fashion magazine.

Nina closed her eyes, listening to the rain and wind

beating against the building, and wondered how long it would be before they could telephone for help. She opened her eyes to find Ross watching her.

'What?'

'You're shattered. Close your eyes again. I'm going to check on our patient and Phil.' He winked at her and then wandered off towards her bedroom.

Nina groaned, closed her eyes, and lowered her head to her folded arms.

Ten years had passed since she'd left Mistake Creek, and she cringed when she thought back to how things had been left between them back then.

They'd dated towards the end of high school, but she'd baulked at the idea of remaining in the small township for the rest of her life. And so, after a few months, she'd broken off their relationship, and although Ross had avoided her for a couple of weeks, they'd managed to patch up their friendship.

At least until Nina had changed her mind three months later, regretting her haste to move on and realising how much she'd missed Ross's company during that time. After spending several weeks attending college interviews, she'd found a course she could study closer to Mistake Creek.

It had been another month until she'd psyched herself up enough to tell Ross. Her passion for him rekindled, she'd returned to the small town, having managed to convince herself he'd still feel the same way.

She'd driven out to the Flanagan farm, timing her

arrival so that Ross and his father were returning to the house after working in the fields all day.

She didn't spot the two-door coupe parked next to the house until afterwards. If she had, she would have turned around.

Instead, she'd parked next to Ross's truck, climbed out and hurried across to where Ross and his father were walking with three of their dogs from a field. Ross's father had closed the gate and excused himself, disappearing across the yard and into the large homestead to leave Nina and Ross alone.

She'd turned to him then, her blood rushing through her veins as she opened her mouth to speak the words she'd spent days rehearsing.

When she'd told him that she loved him, he'd taken a step back, confusion etched across his face, and then he'd looked down at his feet.

'I'm sorry, Nina,' he'd murmured. 'You didn't want me, remember? You left. You're too late.'

Her brain had taken a moment to register her shock, but before she could speak, the door to the property had swung open, and a female voice had called over to them.

'Ross – your mother says dinner's nearly ready. Are you coming in?'

Nina had spun round to see a woman standing at the threshold, her hand shading her eyes from the setting sun. Her golden hair curled over her shoulders, and she already looked at home as she smiled at Ross.

Nina had fled, running back to her car before Ross could say another word or, worse, invite her to stay for dinner out of politeness.

As she drove back towards the truck stop, tears had coursed down her cheeks. Why had it taken so long for her to realize how she felt? How could she have been so stupid as to ruin their friendship?

She'd pulled the vehicle to the side of the road, unable to drive as wracking sobs consumed her.

She'd managed to pull her phone from her bag and call her father, to tell him she needed somewhere to stay the night. She'd then climbed out to sit on the hood of the car, watching the sun set over the fields, lost in thought, deliberately deleting each of the text messages that Ross sent, asking her to call him.

She'd eventually reached the truck stop, parking the car at the rear of the property, before pushing open the back door and stumbling into the kitchen.

Her father had turned from the small stove, anguish in his eyes.

'Thank God you're here,' he'd said, pulling her into a hug. 'Ross phoned me and said you'd left the farm in a bit of a state. He was worried about you, especially when you didn't answer his calls.'

He'd waited until Nina's sobs had subsided, and then told her that the woman was someone Ross had met at an agricultural conference two months before. She'd been a regular visitor to the Flanagans at Mistake Creek ever since.

'She looked so at home,' Nina had said, wiping angrily at her eyes, her chest aching.

Shock, disbelief, and confusion had clouded her thoughts over the subsequent days, and she'd studiously avoided Ross and the farm. She'd spurned her father's attempts to coax her to talk to Ross and rekindle their friendship, until one morning she announced to him that she was accepting a college place at San Francisco instead, and fled.

In the intervening years, she'd heard that Ross had married the woman, Stephanie, but that it had only lasted a few years, as Stephanie realized the life of a farmer's wife in drought-stricken California wasn't for her.

Nina opened her eyes, sat up, and ran her hand through her hair. There'd be enough time to face up to her past – and the fact the business was for sale and she'd be returning to the city again – once the storm had passed and the events of the past few hours were behind her.

She twisted on her chair in time to see Dani throw the magazine aside with a growl.

'Are you okay?'

The woman's head shot up, and Nina noticed her harried look before she plastered a smile across her face.

'Yes, thanks. Sorry—I'm not very good at being cooped up.' She waved her hand in the air. 'And storms make me nervous.'

Nina wandered over to the threadbare sofa and sat down. 'I guess I'm a bit the same,' she said. 'I mean, I've been living in the city for the past ten years, but I can't remember the last time the valley had a storm like this, even when I was a kid.'

Sean reappeared, drying his hands on a towel. A door slammed shut towards the back of the property, and he glanced over his shoulder before dumping the towel on the counter and joining the two women.

Dani eased back into the sofa and curled her legs under her. 'What do you do in the city?'

Nina sighed. 'I've just lost my job. I was an administrator at a law firm.'

'A law firm? What did you do there?'

'Mostly sorting out the court paperwork, but they got taken over by a larger firm, so if I can sell this place I can look after my father. I'll find something else to do once he's settled.' Nina yawned, then stood up and eased out the cricks in her shoulders. 'What about you?'

'Oh, not much these days. I help Sean with his business. We decided to take a break recently, so we've spent the last week on the road.' Dani groaned and shifted in her seat. 'Which is why I'm saddle sore – it's been a while since I've been on a motorbike.'

Nina laughed. 'Me too – I used to ride dirt bikes with Ross and his brother over at their farm during the summer holidays. I'd probably be sore if I had to ride for a week now.'

She frowned at the sound of Ross calling her name from the direction of her bedroom.

A second shout galvanized her into action.

'Get in here, quick!'

She sprinted past the counter, her feet sliding on the tiled floor as she rounded the corner, and ran down the passageway towards her bedroom, the beam from her flashlight bouncing off the walls.

She slowed her momentum. Clutching the doorframe, she peered round, her brow creasing as she saw Ross crouched on the floor next to the prone truck driver, his face fearful in the light from his discarded flashlight.

'I think Phil's dead,' he said, his arms jerking as he applied pressure to the other man's chest. 'He's not breathing, and I can't get him to respond.'

TWELVE

Nina dropped to the floor on the other side of Phil's body and motioned to Ross to move aside so they could split the chest compressions between them.

'What happened?' she asked, her own heart racing as her hands pumped Phil's chest.

'I don't know,' Ross said. 'I came back to check on our wounded guest, and Phil was fine. Looked a bit sleepy from the alcohol, and tired, but that's all.'

He stopped, leaned forward, and motioned to her that she should let him take over once more.

'I thought he was sleeping,' he said. 'Then the back door slammed – I figured I'd forgotten to lock it. I went to shut it. When I came back, he was on the floor. I thought he'd passed out from the drink.'

Nina pushed him away. 'Let me – you're tiring.'

Neither of them spoke as she worked, the only sound in the room that of their breathing.

Nina's mind raced as she flexed her palms and concentrated on the compressions. She couldn't understand why Phil would be okay one minute, then in a state of collapse moments later. She became aware of footsteps, a flashlight beam against the opposite wall, then movement behind her.

'Anything we can do?'

Sean's voice cut through her concentration.

Nina looked over her shoulder at him, her hands still working, then back to Ross, who was holding his fingers against Phil's neck, moving them across the skin, his jaw set.

'What's going on?'

Dani joined them, the note of concern in her voice cutting through the tension in the room.

'Go and try the landline,' said Ross. 'See if you can get through to the emergency services. Tell them it looks like Phil's had a heart attack.'

'My cell phone's on top of it,' added Nina. 'Try that, too.'

Dani's footsteps receded as she ran from the room, closely followed by Sean.

'Do you think they'll get through?' asked Nina, her arms aching from the exertion.

He shrugged. 'We have to try.'

His hands moved from Phil's neck and wrapped around

the man's wrist. He shook his head and moved his hands until he covered Nina's, seeking out her fingers in the near darkness.

'Stop. It's too late. He's gone.'

'He can't be.' Nina kept pumping her hands on the man's chest, her hair rocking across her face with the motion. 'We can't give up yet.'

'Nina, there's no pulse. We've been doing this for ten minutes straight,' Ross murmured. 'He's dead.'

'The phone line's still down. And there's no signal on any of the phones.' Sean's voice echoed through the building towards them.

A ragged breath escaped Nina's lips as she stopped the compressions and leaned back on her heels.

Somehow, she'd known it had been a hopeless task. Phil's body had been unresponsive, his eyes closed and his face impassive in the light from her torch the entire time they'd been working on him.

She raised her head, the sound of Ross's breathing closing the gap between them. He sounded as exhausted as she felt as she tried to keep her composure. She remained still, her thoughts churning, wondering whether they could've done more if they'd found Phil sooner.

Dani's voice cut through the silence as she peered around the doorframe, the beam from her flashlight bobbing around on the carpet next to Phil's feet.

'I wish we'd never come back here,' she hissed. 'We should've kept going to town.'

Nina turned, and squinted as the light struck her in the face. She raised her hand to shield her eyes.

Sean's voice silenced Dani as he ushered her from the room, talking to her in undertones.

Nina sighed, reached forward, and began to re-button Phil's shirt, then frowned.

'Are you okay?'

'Hang on.' She leaned forward and brushed her fingertips through Phil's hair, then held up her hand. Blood covered her fingers.

Ross's eyes widened.

'I don't think he had a heart attack,' said Nina, her voice shaking. She glanced at Phil's still body, then back to the bed. 'Do you think he killed him?' she whispered.

'He looks pretty out of it still,' said Ross.

'He could be pretending.'

'Or Phil could've hit his head when he fell,' said Ross. 'It could be as simple an explanation as that.'

Nina stood and walked over to the pile of towels they'd used earlier and wiped Phil's blood from her fingers.

What if Ross was right? What if Phil had simply had a heart attack, and had hit his head as he'd collapsed to the floor?

She swallowed. What if Ross was lying?

The Ross she'd grown up with would never have hurt another person. Was it really possible for someone to change so much?

'Hey.' He rose and moved towards her. 'Are you okay?'

She nodded and sniffled. 'Fine.'

'Come here.'

Ross offered her his hand.

She slipped her fingers between his, and he pulled her closer before his arms enveloped her.

'You've had one hell of a shock. We both have.'

She closed her eyes and rested her forehead against his chest, grateful for the gesture.

'This day couldn't possibly get any worse,' she mumbled into his shirt.

'Tell me about it.'

His chest rose and fell under the weight of her head, and she wrinkled her nose at the scent of his sweat before realising she'd also worked as hard as him that day.

She pushed away and looked up at him.

'Okay?'

She nodded. 'Yes. Thanks.'

'Okay. I'm going to go over to the accommodation block. See if I can find a spare blanket.'

Nina opened her mouth to ask why before the realisation hit her. She bit her lip.

'It's the best we can do for him at the moment,' said Ross. 'He'd understand.'

'I know.'

She looked down at Phil, then to the motionless

wounded man in her bed. Something still didn't feel right. She gestured to Ross to step outside the room.

'What is it?' His brow creased as he leaned against the wall, his arms crossed.

Nina held a finger to her lips. 'Keep your voice down,' she whispered. She craned her neck round the doorframe to check on the injured stranger and then turned back to Ross. 'Don't you think it's a bit strange, Phil having a heart attack?'

'What do you mean?'

She shrugged. 'He's not that old.'

'Driving a truck isn't exactly a healthy lifestyle.'

'I know – but he didn't show any symptoms, did he?'

'Sometimes heart attacks happen like that, don't they? I mean, I'm not a medical expert, but you hear stories of perfectly healthy people with no medical history of heart problems just dropping dead one day, don't you?'

'Yeah.' Nina bit her lip.

'What?' Ross stepped closer, lowering his voice. 'What are you thinking?'

'Nothing – it's stupid.'

'Come on. This is me you're talking to,' said Ross. 'Tell me.'

Nina exhaled loudly, ignoring the liquid sensation in her lungs, wondering how much she should tell him. She decided to play safe. 'What if the wounded man *did* attack him?'

She stepped back as Ross's eyebrows shot upwards.

He stepped sideways and checked the stranger was still asleep, then turned back to Nina, grabbed her arm and pulled her along the corridor until they were closer to the back door.

'Are you serious?' he spluttered.

'Did you happen to notice if he moved between you leaving the room to check the back door, and coming back?'

'No.' Ross bit his lip. 'No, when I went back into the room, Phil was on the floor and I started CPR on him.' He cursed. 'I didn't even look at our guest.'

Nina noted the sarcasm in his voice and held up her hand to placate him. 'It's just a thought, that's all.'

'Well, you're wrong.' He exhaled loudly. 'You must be. I mean, he wouldn't have had time to do anything to Phil.'

'How long did you leave the room for?'

Ross rubbed his hand across the back of his neck. 'Five minutes, max. I walked out of the room, opened the back door, checked outside to make sure everything was okay out there, then closed it and locked it. Then I went to the bathroom and took a piss. Five minutes. It couldn't have been more than that.'

Nina sighed, reached out, and ran her hand down Ross's arm. 'I'm sorry. You're right,' she said. 'I'm so wound up about being back here, and what's happened.' She forced a laugh, but it came out breathless. 'I'm getting paranoid.'

A smile crossed Ross's lips, but it didn't reach his eyes.

'I'll go and find that blanket,' he said. 'You'd better check on our other guests.'

Nina stepped aside as he unlocked the back door and stepped into the pouring rain before she wandered back towards the front of the building. As she passed her bedroom, she couldn't help looking at Phil's body.

She frowned, then quietly slipped into the room and crouched down next to him. She checked over her shoulder, and then at the figure on the bed, before reaching out and gently turning Phil's head.

She bit back an exclamation as she saw the wound to the back of the man's skull.

It was deep, deeper than she'd realized when she'd found blood in Phil's hair moments earlier. As if he'd been taken by surprise, hit from behind with a blunt weapon.

She moved his head back and stood, moving swiftly to the door. Stepping back into the passageway, she gripped the doorframe and stared at the prone figure.

Was Ross telling the truth?

Had he really left the room to check the back door? She'd heard it slam in its frame, but what if Ross had done that on purpose, to cover his tracks?

She shook her head to clear the thought.

Why would Ross kill Phil? He had nothing to hide – did he?

Her gaze traveled over the mound of bedding covering

the stranger. She couldn't recall if he was in the same position they'd left him in.

Had he moved?

She stepped around Phil's body towards the bed. Breathing hard, she reached out and touched his arm.

He didn't move.

'Wake up,' she hissed, and squeezed his arm.

He didn't react, and she watched as his chest rose and fell as if he were in a deep sleep.

She bit her lip. If he wasn't asleep, then he was a good actor – she knew his shoulder must be hurting him, so if he wasn't unconscious, would he have had time to murder Phil before returning to the bed and feigning sleep?

The sound of Sean and Dani's voices further along the passageway roused her from her thoughts. They sounded like they were arguing again.

She hurried back to the front of the truck stop, chewing her fingernail, unconvinced now that Phil had simply succumbed to a heart attack, and wondered which of the three men in the truck stop with her had murdered him.

THIRTEEN

Ross ran across the narrow footpath that separated the back of the truck stop and the accommodation block.

Fumbling with the keys, his hands shaking, he finally found the master key and unlocked the first room.

He stepped inside and breathed out a sigh of relief, thankful for the separate power source as the lights flickered to life when he flipped the switch.

The room was sparse, with only a double bed, side tables, and a wardrobe filling the space. Another door at the rear of the room led to a small bathroom. A tired brown carpet covered the floor, while the lighting did little to hide the fact the paintwork needed updating.

Nina's father had designed the rooms to be functional, nothing more, his reasoning being that most people only stayed for a night, for convenience rather than a desire to remain in Mistake Creek for any longer than was necessary.

Ross stepped across to the wardrobe, pulled open the doors, and began to grab the spare linen off the top shelf, his mind working overtime.

Somehow, he had to get Nina away from the truck stop – and fast.

He'd had his suspicions about the motorcyclist and his wife earlier in the evening, when they'd been so vague in their explanation to Nina about where they'd traveled and where they were headed.

He moved quickly, not wanting to leave Nina alone with them longer than he had to.

When she'd discovered blood in the man's hair, his first thought had been that it was because Phil had hit his head as he'd slumped to the floor. Except that when he'd lifted his flashlight to search the room for something to cover his body with, he'd noticed Sean standing at the doorway, a strange look in his eyes as the beam had swept over his face.

Since then, he'd been convinced the motorcyclist had murdered him.

Only he didn't have any proof. Not yet.

And he didn't want to frighten Nina.

He cursed as his thoughts returned to the injured man who had slept through the commotion.

He'd checked over his shoulder each time Nina had taken over the compressions, but there had been no movement, no indication the man even knew they were there.

Either he was really unconscious from his wound, or he was a very good actor.

But why? Was he the killer? What was he hiding?

Or who was he hiding from?

Folding a blanket across his arm, Ross closed the wardrobe and stalked back to the door, his jaw clenched.

He recalled the way Nina had looked at him before he'd stepped outside. It was obvious to him that she suspected something wasn't right about the situation.

A sickness threatened to overwhelm him as another thought struck him.

When she had discovered the blood, he'd done his best to alleviate her fears. In hindsight, he realized he should've told her he thought the same as she – that Phil had been murdered.

Instead, she now suspected him as well. He could see it in her eyes.

Did she think he was capable of murder? Is that why she clammed up suddenly?

He moved towards the made-up bed, its mattress sagging under his weight. Dropping the blankets on the counterpane, he leaned forward and held his head in his hands. A groan escaped his lips.

Why did Nina have to return to Mistake Creek this week? He knew her father had been showing signs of dementia – hell, he'd been the one who had rushed to

Clint's aid when townspeople phoned the Flanagan property to say they were worried about their neighbour.

He remembered the call his own father made to Nina, telling her she needed to return, after Ross had baulked at the prospect of speaking to her without it being face-to-face after all this time.

Yet, until this evening's frightening scenario, it had been good to see her after so long apart. They'd fallen into their old habits within hours of working together to fix up the property.

He punched the mattress in frustration.

He had to solve this if he was going to prove his own innocence to her.

He thought about the injury to Phil's head. Something blunt had to have caused it. His head jerked up, and he squinted through the rain towards the outbuilding where he and Sean had stored the motorbike.

Had Sean killed Phil?

He stood, grabbed the blankets, and straightened his shoulders, then headed for the door, his decision made.

All he had to do was find what had been used to kill Phil, without the other two men in the truck stop finding out what he was up to.

And before Nina jumped to the wrong conclusion and publicly accused him of murder.

Ross hurried across the footpath towards the truck stop, shut the back door, and pocketed the key, then sped along the passageway towards Nina's bedroom.

He could hear her talking with Sean and Dani in the front room of the truck stop, her calming tones disguising any fear she might be suffering.

He gripped the blanket and hoped she'd keep their guests distracted long enough for him to take a look around the room.

He shook out the blanket and draped it over Phil's body, avoiding having to look at the man's face, then turned, his hands on his hips, wondering where to start.

The blow to Phil's head had been savage, and likely caused by a heavy object to have killed him outright.

Ross moved to the bedside table and reached out to the lamp placed on it.

Its brass base shone in the flashlight's beam as he picked it up and checked its edges. No tell-tale signs of blood remained, not even a smear.

He replaced it and cursed under his breath.

Next, he moved to the other side of the bed and checked the sports bag he'd left against the wall. It remained zipped up, just as he'd left it, no evidence of being tampered with, so he discounted its contents as potential murder weapons for the time being.

He spun round as Nina's voice rose, a chair scraped across tiles, and he realized he was running out of time.

He moved back to the doorway, checked no-one was approaching, and then moved between Phil's body and the bed.

Kneeling, he lifted the counterpane and swung his

flashlight back and forth under the bed. On the second sweep, he found what he'd been looking for.

He reached out, then changed his mind at the last second and tugged his shirtsleeve over his hand before pulling the object towards him.

A flashlight, identical to his.

Except that on this one, the rim around the bulb had been stained a rusty shade of red.

Ross fought down bile at the sight of black hairs embedded in the congealed liquid, then spun round at footsteps outside the door, and froze.

FOURTEEN

'Ross? What's wrong?'

Nina leaned against the doorframe and tried to see what Ross was doing.

He held a second flashlight in his hands, a frown creasing his brow. He jumped when she spoke.

'Close the door,' he said, moving towards her.

She slipped into the room and pushed the door shut. 'What's going on?'

Ross held the flashlight up to her. 'I think we're in trouble.'

'What do you mean?'

He didn't answer and instead pointed to the rim.

Nina moved closer, then saw the red stain at its edge and lowered her gaze to the blanket on the floor. 'Is that... is that *blood*?'

'I think so,' he murmured. 'I think Phil was killed.'

'*Murdered*?'

'Shh,' Ross hissed. His hand shot out and covered Nina's mouth. 'Keep your voice down!'

She nodded, and he lowered his hand.

'Why would someone kill Phil?' demanded Nina. 'What the hell is going on around here?'

'I don't know,' he said. 'Unless it's to do with that body he said he found up by the creek.'

Nina's gaze fell to the unconscious man lying prone on the bed. He hadn't moved the whole time they'd been talking. But what if he was pretending?

'Do – do you think he did it?' she whispered.

'I don't think so,' said Ross. 'He seems pretty much out of it.' He walked round to the other side of the bed.

'So, it must be Sean?' Nina said. Then paused. *What if Ross was the killer?*

Their eyes met, and he began to shake his head.

'It wasn't me, Nina.'

She began to back away from him. 'Stay there, Ross.'

'Nina, please – listen to me,' he said, kicking the bag by the bed out of his way. He started to move towards her. 'You've got to believe me. I had nothing to do with this.'

'Stay away from me!'

Nina stepped back, until her fingers touched the door handle, then cried out as the door moved under her body weight, pushing her forwards.

It opened, and Sean peered into the room.

'Is everything okay? We heard voices.'

'It's fine, really,' said Ross, his voice calm. 'We were just talking.'

Nina's gaze moved from Ross, then back to Sean.

Something in Ross's expression frightened her, and she wondered when he'd learned to lie so easily.

'Th-that's right,' she stammered. 'We were wondering how long this storm is going to last for.' She forced a smile. 'It's been a while since either of us can remember one as bad as this.'

'Okay.' Sean's eyes flickered back to Ross, then to the torch in his hand.

Nina saw his jaw tighten and acted on instinct.

She shoved herself against him, and, caught off balance, he staggered back through the open door, his face contorted with anger.

She slammed the door shut and then panicked as the handle twisted and the door began to move against her weight. 'Ross!'

'Here!'

He joined her at the door, slipping the chair underneath the handle. Breathing hard, he narrowed his eyes at her.

'You okay? What happened there?'

She shook her head. 'I don't know – something about the way he looked at you. He saw the flashlight in your hand.'

Sean began to hammer on the door, his fists thundering on the thin wood.

'This isn't going to hold for long,' whispered Nina,

running her hands over the surface. 'What are we going to do?'

'I think we found our murderer,' said Ross.

'I think you're right – but why kill Phil? Because he found the other body?'

Ross nodded. 'And he was asking a lot of questions. Maybe they got spooked.'

'You think Dani is involved too?'

'She must be – there's no other explanation, is there?'

'Would you two mind keeping the noise down? I'm trying to think.'

Nina spun round.

The stranger was rubbing a hand over his eyes.

'Excuse me?'

He lowered his hand. 'I said, keep the noise down.' He paused when Nina glared at him. 'Please.'

He grimaced and clasped a hand to his injured shoulder.

'What the hell is going on?' Nina strode over to the bed. 'Did you kill Phil?'

'No.'

'Then why on earth didn't you help him?'

'I couldn't,' said the man. He sighed. 'If I had, I would've blown any chance I've got to get you and Ross away from here.'

Nina opened her mouth to speak, but then realized Sean had stopped banging on the door. 'I think he's gone.'

'He'll be back.' The man looked away from her. 'How are you holding up, Ross?'

'Like shit.' Ross checked the chair would hold the door handle before joining them. 'You know John?'

'He's my partner. We got split up. I got stabbed.'

'How did we do patching you up?'

'I hurt like hell. Had worse, though.' He eased himself up until he was sitting. 'Did John give you anything to look after, for emergencies?'

'There's a bag under the bed – far side.'

Nina watched as the man stretched across the width of the bed until he could reach the sports bag.

'We've got to go, people. Get ready to move out,' he said. 'Where did you put your rifle, Ross?'

'On the counter.'

'Not good.'

He pulled out a t-shirt and a cotton shirt from the sports bag and eased them over his shoulder.

Nina spun round to face Ross. 'What's going on?'

'I'll explain later,' he said, refusing to meet her gaze. 'I promise.'

The stranger said nothing and instead returned his attention to the sports bag. His hands reappeared, a large gun in one and a magazine of ammunition in the other. 'Are the phones working?'

'There are no cell phone signals, and the landline's gone down.'

The stranger swung his legs over the bed, checked the safety on his gun, and leaned forward.

'What the hell are you doing?'

'Saving you.' He stood, swaying on his feet, and she reached out to steady him. 'Thanks.'

'You're welcome.'

He grinned, appearing to ignore the note of sarcasm in her voice. 'Now you're catching on.' He moved to the window and peered out into the night. 'Is there a back door out of here?'

Nina nodded. 'Yes. Why?'

''Cause we're not going out the front door. I'll run out of ammunition if we try to shoot our way out of here.' He turned and snatched up the flashlight from where Ross had dropped it onto the bed, and tucked it down his shirt. 'You know the layout of the place, Ross?'

'Yes.' Ross held his hand up, jangling the keys. 'And the back door is locked.'

'Good.' The stranger glared at Nina to stop her from interrupting. 'Did you hear that?'

She shook her head mutely, glancing at Ross.

'Voices. They're coming back.' The stranger hurried towards the door and put his ear to the surface, then spun round. 'We're not going to make it in time. What's below that window?'

'Trash cans.'

'Perfect.' He moved to the window and peered out into

116

the darkness, then gripped the frame and pulled. It didn't move.

'It's been stuck for years,' said Nina.

The stranger grunted, tried once more, and then gave up. 'Ross, grab that chair. On my count, smash the window.' He checked over his shoulder. 'Nina, fold that blanket up and bring it over here. As soon as he breaks the window, drop it over the sill and get out. Okay?'

'Okay.' Nina crouched and hefted the blanket away from Phil's body, averting her eyes from the dead man's face. She folded the covering and joined the stranger and Ross by the window.

'Do you have a jacket in that wardrobe?' he asked.

'Yes, why?'

'Go put it on – quickly. You'll need it out there.'

Nina handed Ross the blanket, dashed across the room, and pulled her leather jacket off its hanger. Two of her father's old work coats swung next to it. She grabbed them and threw one to Ross, the other to the stranger.

'Let's do this,' he said. He held Nina back. 'Turn your head away,' he said. 'Okay, Ross. Three. Two. One!'

The crash from the wooden chair hitting the windowpanes exploded round the room.

'Now!' The stranger used the butt of his gun to smash the remnants of glass from the frame.

Nina moved, throwing the blanket across the jagged shards in the sill.

'Go,' he urged.

She scrambled through the opening and landed between two steel trash cans, knocking them to the ground.

As a lightning bolt streaked through the sky, she scuttled out of the way and cowered next to the wall, her thoughts in turmoil as she tried to process what was happening to her.

A man lay dead on her bedroom floor, probably murdered. A stranger who had appeared at her doorstep covered in blood was now pushing her through her own bedroom window, urging her to hurry, and he was armed with the biggest handgun she'd ever seen.

She jumped as Ross tumbled through the window beside her, fell into a crouch, and flattened his body to the wall, before the stranger's face appeared at the window.

'Everyone okay?'

They both nodded.

'Good. Help me here.'

She joined Ross at the window and helped the other man scramble to safety. Her eyes opened wide as an axe head smashed through her bedroom door behind him.

'Move it, people, or we're going to have company real soon.'

Nina cowered as a blast emanated from the back of the truck stop.

With one final effort, the stranger landed on the ground next to them.

'I think they just found out the back door's locked,' said Ross, his voice shaking.

'And they've got your rifle,' said the stranger.

'What do we do?' Nina searched Ross's face for answers, but he looked as scared as she felt.

Instead the stranger stood, handed Nina a dustbin lid, and pointed across the concrete hardstand.

'Head for the biggest vehicle to give us some cover. No sense in getting trapped in one of the outbuildings if we can't call for help.'

Nina grabbed the lid from him. 'And this?'

'A bit of protection in case they start firing at us before we get there.' He shrugged. 'It might work.' He turned to Ross. 'Don't stop running, understand?'

'Yeah.'

Nina's heart lurched as Ross's eyes opened wide and he began to yell; at the same time a splintering crash emanated from her bedroom.

'Run! Come on!'

The man behind her didn't hesitate.

He shoved her hard, sending her stumbling towards Ross, who grabbed her hand and pulled her after him.

She heard Sean curse, then a loud explosion as he fired the rifle.

'Go! Go!' yelled the stranger.

Nina shrieked and then concentrated on keeping pace with Ross, their feet squelching into the soft layer of mud that now covered the walkway between the truck stop and the vehicles.

Nina stumbled across the forecourt between the two

men, her feet sending up a spray of water as she tried to keep up with them, her arm aching from being pulled along by Ross.

The stranger matched Ross's pace, but Nina noticed how he held his hand against his shoulder, and she imagined the droplets running down his face were sweat as well as the rain that beat down on them.

A flash of lightning crossed the sky, illuminating the forecourt and the vehicles parked under the canopy. Nina cried out in terror, momentarily certain they'd be struck by a lightning bolt, seconds before thunder echoed around the valley.

Ross pulled her down behind his pick-up truck, their breathing audible over the deluge of water around them.

Nina tried to catch his attention, to seek reassurance, but the stranger slid to a stop beside them, squatted down, and aimed his weapon back towards the truck stop. Although Nina and Ross gasped for breath, she noticed the stranger appeared enlivened by the shocking turn of events, despite his injury.

'Everyone okay?' he asked.

Nina recoiled as a lightning bolt struck the ground less than a mile away. The sound wave reached her a split second later, the resounding crack of electricity ripping through the air.

'Y-yes,' Nina managed. 'I'm okay.'

'Good.' The stranger shifted his weight, and jutted his chin towards the back of the pick-up truck. 'Get yourself down that end, Ross. We'll try to put some more space between us and them.'

Nina watched as Ross ran in a crouch along the length of the vehicle. When he got there, he checked over his shoulder at her.

She opened her mouth to call to him, to let him know that she'd join him, when gunfire roared from the direction of the truck stop.

She ducked instinctively, and turned to the stranger.

He used a hand to signal to her to keep her head down, then peered over her, back towards the buildings, and fired four shots in quick succession.

A roll of thunder echoed the last bullet, the rumbling echoing in Nina's chest.

A moment's silence preceded a loud curse, and then Sean's voice cut across the forecourt.

'You've got ten seconds to show yourselves, or I'll kill you all!' he yelled.

'What do we do?' cried Nina.

'I don't know,' Ross shouted, and looked to the man next to Nina for help.

The stranger chuckled under his breath.

'Jesus,' he drawled as he readied his weapon. He slid a fresh magazine into his gun.

'Looks like it's going to be up to me to get you out of the shit, doesn't it?'

FIFTEEN

Nina's jaw dropped at the excitement in his eyes. It scared her, and she looked to the man behind her for reassurance. 'Ross? What's going on?'

In reply, he shuffled back towards her and pushed her to the wet concrete next to the truck's door. 'Keep down.'

The two men crouched beside her, and Ross turned to the stranger. 'Now what do we do?'

'The phones definitely weren't working?'

'No.'

'Shit.' The stranger punched the side panel of the truck. 'Okay. We couldn't have foreseen this. Plan B then. We'll drive as far as the creek. Hopefully there's still some equipment left in John's car we can use.'

Nina's attention moved from one man to the other as they spoke, her mind racing. Ross and the stranger were talking as if they knew each other, as if they'd been

122

expecting something like this to happen tonight. She glared at the stranger.

'Who *are* you?'

'Nina, this is Special Agent Kyle Roberts,' said Ross. 'He's with the FBI. I was helping his partner, John.'

'FBI?' She began to stand. 'What the *hell* is going on here?'

In reply, the FBI agent placed his hand on her shoulder and pulled her down. 'We'll explain later. Right now, we have to get out of here.'

He pushed her out of the way, and she watched as Ross reached into his jeans pocket and pulled out the keys to the truck, his hands shaking. He caught her staring at him, and his lips pursed.

'Not quite the welcome home you were expecting, right?'

Nina remained silent, shocked at how little she knew about the man standing in front of her.

What was he doing with the FBI?

And what the hell was the FBI doing in Mistake Creek?

Next to her, Kyle's head flicked towards the truck stop, a second before she felt his weight against her.

She looked to see what had caught his attention and shrieked. Sean stood in the doorway, the rifle in his hands.

'Get down!'

The report from the weapon echoed into the night.

123

Nina swore as the two men landed on top of her, protecting her from the onslaught.

A strong hand wrapped around Nina's arm and she was half-pulled, half-pushed by the two men until they'd reached the opposite side of the truck, out of firing line from the truck stop.

Kyle grunted as they hit the ground and then yelled in her ear.

'Okay, move!'

He fired his gun over his shoulder as they ran side by side towards the next vehicle.

A split second later, another shot blasted at them, and they ducked for cover behind the next truck.

Nina's ears rang from the noise, but she heard a muffled cry from Ross and looked up to see him leaning against the back of the truck, clutching his leg.

'No!'

Nina shoved against Kyle's weight, fighting to untangle herself from his limbs to reach Ross.

A mask of pain contorted his features, and she noticed his face had gone a sickly pale color.

Kyle hauled her down, holding her against his body until she stopped thrashing, then pulled her with him, and they crawled the few paces to where Ross lay.

'How bad is it?' asked the FBI agent. 'Is it deep?'

'I can't look,' said Ross.

'Here, let me.'

Nina watched in horror as Kyle prised Ross's

fingers away from the wound and exposed a bloodied mess of skin and denim. A large dark stain of blood bloomed over his jeans, splinters of white bone protruding from the wound. She whimpered, her gaze meeting his.

'What about my truck?' Ross hissed.

Kyle moved carefully to the passenger door and slowly raised his head. He ducked back down and crawled to where Nina and Ross waited. 'That first blast tore a hole in the front tire,' he said.

'Shit.'

'What about the other one?' asked Nina. 'Can't we take that instead?'

'No,' said Kyle. 'It's too exposed. We'd have to cross right in front of the building to get to it. We'd be dead within seconds.'

Ross groaned, tried to shift his leg, and cried out in pain.

'This is bad,' Kyle murmured. 'We can't move you like this.' He cursed, clutching his shoulder. 'How the *hell* did our cover get blown?'

Nina leaned towards the FBI agent. 'You're bleeding again.'

He grimaced and lifted his hand off his shoulder, as if noticing the fresh blood for the first time.

'I'm not surprised,' he said. 'You landed on me.'

Nina glared at him.

'Can you get her away from here?' asked Ross.

Nina opened her mouth to protest, but he ignored her and continued.

'Quick. They'll soon realize we're not moving and will be over here to make sure they finish the job. You can't have much ammunition left, right?'

'Two rounds in this. One more clip.'

'Ross, no – we can't leave you!' Nina spun on her knees to face Kyle, her hair plastered to her skin. 'We have to take him with us!'

He ignored her, ducked as another bolt of lightning tore across the sky, and kept his focus on the other man.

'You know what you're saying, right?'

Ross nodded, his hands clutching his leg.

Nina watched him set his jaw before he spoke again.

'She can't help both of us – your shoulder's getting worse, and you're the only one who knows how to get the back-up we need. If you try to carry me, I'll slow you down – we'll all get killed.' He looked at Nina as he spoke. 'Keep her safe for me.'

Kyle reached into his pocket and drew out the last clip, discarded the spent one and slotted the replacement into the weapon. 'Give us some cover to get to the barn if you can.' He reached out and squeezed Ross's shoulder, then handed him his gun. 'Keep this other one for you, okay?' he said, handing over the clip with two bullets. 'I'll do whatever it takes to get her out of here, I promise.'

Ross nodded, his face pale.

Kyle turned to Nina. 'Okay, let's go.'

She shook her head. 'I can't — we can't leave him here!'

'Go with him, Nina,' said Ross. 'It'll be okay.'

Tears pricked at her eyes, then escaped and showered her cheeks. 'It won't be okay,' she said. She angrily wiped the tears away with her sleeve.

'We're running out of time.'

She looked up at the touch of Kyle's hand on her shoulder.

'We need to move now.'

'Where are we going?'

'That outbuilding, over there.'

'We'll never make it!'

'Don't look back,' he said. 'Just go.'

'But Ross…'

'We can't help him. We need to move. *Now*.'

SIXTEEN

Nina's arm was almost wrenched from its socket as Kyle hauled her over the rain-lashed forecourt, racing towards the large outbuilding that marked the boundary to the property.

She sensed, rather than heard, the gunshots that reverberated around her as Ross tried to provide cover fire.

She'd never been so terrified.

Kyle slid to a stop by the outbuilding and threw his weight against the door.

They stumbled, panting, into the dark space before he slammed the door shut, shoving the steel bolts across the wooden frame.

Nina pushed her back to the hard surface of the shed wall and slicked her wet hair off her face. 'I can't do this.'

Kyle turned from the doors and in two strides crossed

the shed to her. 'You haven't got a choice,' he said. 'There's no other way.'

Her gaze flickered to the closed wooden doors. 'He's not shooting anymore. He's out of bullets, right?'

She screamed as an explosion rocked the shed. Kyle forced her to the floor, sheltering her body with his.

The sound reverberated around the enclosed space before dissipating.

She raised her head to look over Kyle's shoulder and shuddered at the gaping hole in the doors.

'*Now* do you believe me?'

She bit her lip, trying to work through the myriad of emotions running through her mind.

'He's dangerous – that's Ross's rifle, right?' said Kyle.

She nodded.

'So we have to move. *Now.*'

He pulled her up with him, dragging her to the back of the shed. 'I'm presuming there's a back door?'

She pointed, not trusting her voice to remain steady enough to give directions.

'Right, good – come on.'

He grabbed her hand and began leading her through the myriad of discarded machinery and storage boxes.

'Wait.' She dug in her heels and forced him to stop.

'What?'

'If he's got a rifle, and you're injured, we're not going to outrun it, are we?'

'Have you got any better ideas?' He folded his arms and glared at her.

'Yes.' She pointed behind him.

The gleaming metalwork of the motorbike stood sentinel next to the door.

Kyle grinned. 'Good thinking. Can you ride?'

'Yes. Can you?'

His smile disappeared as his gaze fell to his bandaged shoulder. 'Guess I'm pillion.'

'Come on.' She hurried over to the machine and ran her hand over the chrome handlebars, then swore under her breath.

'What's wrong?'

'No keys.'

'Here, let me.'

She stood aside as Kyle bent down to the bike and pulled out a plastic casing containing three wires.

'Can you find a piece of loose wire in here? Something I can hook around these?'

Nina ran over to the workbench in the corner and sifted through discarded tools and debris until she found a short length of electrical wire.

'Will this do?'

Kyle took it from her and twirled it between his fingers. 'Perfect.' He lowered his head to the side of the bike and pulled the wires from the plastic casing, then poked one end of the electrical wire into place. He glanced up at Nina. 'You realize when this starts up, we've got to move fast, right?'

She nodded. 'Yes. Where are we going?'

'Head towards the creek. We'll check John's car, then try to head into town. I need to try to get to a cell phone as soon as possible. I've got to get a message to my field office; otherwise our problems are going to be the least of their worries tonight.'

'What if the creek's flooded? What if we can't get across?'

'Let's concentrate on getting to John's car. There are some things I'm going to need if we're going to survive being out here tonight.'

'Shouldn't we just try and get to the nearest police station? There's one in the town – we could skirt around the creek until we find somewhere to cross.'

'No time,' said Kyle. 'If they find us before I've made my phone call, we're finished anyway. I can't let that happen.'

'But you promised Ross you'd keep me safe – so we should be riding to one of the farms near here, right?'

He dropped the wires from his fingers and stood, a thunderous look etched across his face.

'Lady, I've got more important things on my mind right now than keeping you safe.' He stepped forward and pushed her towards the motorbike, thrusting one of the crash helmets into her hands. 'Get ready.'

She stumbled towards the bike, cursed, and then swung her leg over the saddle and quickly ran her gaze over the dials. She bit her lip. It had been over ten years since she'd ridden, but as she fastened the helmet strap under her chin then reached out and wrapped her fingers round the unfamiliar handlebars, she realized it was too late to back out.

She didn't have a choice.

She raised her head at the sound of the back door to the barn being swung open, and then Kyle jogged back to the bike and bent down to the wires.

'Ready?'

She tapped her foot on the gear lever to make sure the bike was in neutral, flexed her fingers, and then nodded.

'You'd better be,' he growled. 'On three.'

SEVENTEEN

The motorbike engine burst to life with a roar that shook the wooden-slatted walls of the barn.

Nina kept her feet planted firmly on the ground as Kyle launched into the pillion seat, his arms wrapping around her waist.

'Go!' he yelled in her ear.

She flicked her toes against the gear lever, released the clutch, and feathered the back brake, sending the bike shooting forward across the dirt floor.

She cried out in terror as the bike began to slide under her, and then felt the FBI agent shift his weight.

'It's okay – go!' he urged. 'It's just the surface we're on.'

Nina gritted her teeth, flicked the bike into second gear, and held her breath as the machine shot between the open doors of the barn.

As they exited the building, Kyle's hand moved from her waist to her head and pushed down.

'Keep your head down!' he shouted. 'Make yourself a smaller target for them!'

Nina's breath escaped her lips in short gasps, the familiar tightness beginning in her chest.

'Not now,' she murmured, and concentrated on keeping the bike steady as it bounced over the threshold and onto the rain-soaked soil.

Kyle yelled out as the machine lifted off the ground, hitting a pothole, then crashed back to the ground, sending his body lurching into hers.

Nina heard him swearing under his breath and realized he must have knocked his injured shoulder against her.

The motorbike picked up speed, and Nina kicked the gears into third before leaning the machine into a tight right-hand turn, away from the barn and towards the main road.

In her peripheral vision, she could see the bike's owner running from the direction of the main building, the rifle raised, and gritted her teeth. If he fired now—

'Swerve!' yelled Kyle. 'Don't give him an easy target!'

Nina pushed the handlebar on her right, sending the bike into a sharp turn, then left, and zig-zagged her way across the cracked concrete surface of the forecourt.

With each bump, Kyle grunted under his breath, his good arm tightening around her waist.

She heard the first gunshot and cried out in terror. She felt the bike shift under their combined weight and flexed her fingers before easing it into a final right turn, the machine reaching the asphalt of the main road a fraction before she heard the report of a second gunshot in their wake.

Nina straightened the bike, then kicked it into fourth gear and opened the throttle.

They picked up speed quickly, the rain stinging her face as they powered away from the truck stop. All the time, she concentrated on her breathing, her heart hammering as she thought of the man they'd left behind, and wondered how she'd ever forgive herself.

———

Ross had turned his head at the sound of the motorbike's engine roaring to life, his gaze following the two figures huddled together on it as the machine tore across the forecourt of the truck stop and away into the night.

The wind had whipped Nina's hair out from under the helmet, and despite the fear, his mouth had twitched as he imagined the conversation that must have ensued between her and the FBI agent, before the pain from the wound to his leg brought tears to his eyes.

The motorcycle's original owner had shouted from the entrance to the truck stop as the bike had raced past, his swearing carrying across to where Ross sat propped up against the wheel of his pick-up truck, out of sight, firing at Sean to try and distract him.

The sound of the rifle being fired at the escaping couple scared him, but when he heard Sean curse again, he breathed out, relieved to know they'd managed to escape – for now, at least – and his thoughts returned to his own survival.

He twisted until he could see through the truck's cab, calculating whether he'd be able to avoid being seen, in the hope that he could drag himself away from the vehicle and hide while he waited for help to come.

One glance at the holes that had been ripped into the door and dashboard by the rifle blasts told him enough about the success of that idea. He'd be dead the moment he emerged from behind the shelter of the vehicle.

His eyes flickered as he tried to work out if he could crawl and hide somewhere else before Sean found him, but both the outbuildings and the accommodation block were too far.

He discharged the clip from the gun as Kyle had shown him and replaced it with the last magazine, the one with only two bullets. His hands shook with the effort, liquid fire streaming from his leg wound as he tried to concentrate.

Torrents of water ran down his face, and he shifted in the mud to try and keep the dirt from his leg, gasping from the pain that shot through his body.

Between rolls of thunder, he heard footsteps

approaching. He flicked the safety off the weapon and set his shoulders against the vehicle, aiming at the approaching figure from his right.

'Stay where you are!'

Dani's blonde hair became illuminated by the next flash of lightning before the place was thrust into darkness once more.

Her raucous laughter reached him, but her footsteps never wavered.

'Ever shot someone before, Ross?' she called. 'I don't think you have. I don't think you will.'

Ross bit back a curse, removed his other hand from his leg and clutched the gun in a two-handed grip. It still shook.

He pulled the trigger anyway.

And missed.

He heard the thud of the bullet as it hit the wall of the building behind Dani, moments before her laughter reached him.

'Want to try again?' she teased. 'Don't forget to save one for yourself.'

Ross fired, then cried out with frustration as the trigger pulled against an empty magazine. Another tremor seized his body, and he dropped the gun to the ground, clutching his leg in agony.

He removed his hands from the wound, and as blood oozed from between the skin and bone, an idea formed in his mind.

He wiped his hands on his t-shirt where it covered his stomach, the red stains quickly absorbed by the thin cotton fabric.

He gritted his teeth and pressed the wound once more, then wiped his hands on his t-shirt and repeated the motion.

Hot tears mixed with the cold rain running down his cheeks, before he wiped his sleeve across his face.

A sudden movement at his side caught his attention, and he shifted his weight, wrapped his hands around his leg, and groaned.

'Thought I'd find you here.'

Sean moved from the rear of the truck, keeping a wide arc between himself and Ross. He kept the rifle trained on the younger man.

'Where's Hudson?' Ross used his good leg to push himself up into a sitting position against the front wheel and glared at the other man. 'You work with him, don't you?'

Sean shifted the rifle stock against his shoulder. 'No, I work *for* him. Security, if you like. To stop people like you from ruining his plans.' He jerked his head towards the truck stop. 'Although we were just meant to be babysitting the woman to make sure she didn't get in the way.' He chuckled. 'Gave Hudson a near heart attack a few days ago when they discovered this place wasn't completely abandoned like we planned.'

'Why?' Ross pleaded. 'Can't you see what he's doing

138

is wrong? Do you know how many people are going to die?'

The other man shrugged. 'I don't get paid to have an opinion.' He gestured to the gun lying in the mud next to Ross. 'Throw it over here.'

'Have you got him?'

Sean's head twitched up at the sound of Dani's voice carrying across the forecourt, her tone brittle and stressed.

'Yes,' he called back. 'Get your things – we've got to catch up with the bike.'

His gaze flickered back to Ross, the rain trickling down his face and flattening his hair.

Ross swallowed, unable to wrench his eyes away from Sean, until fire ripped through his leg muscles again, and he cried out in pain.

He clutched his stomach, before glaring at the other man. 'You bastard. You shot me!'

'Gut shot as well as the leg, eh? I got lucky.'

Ross held his breath as Sean moved closer, his steps cautious, the weapon pointed at Ross's face.

'Don't shoot him!'

Dani's voice screeched across the forecourt a moment before Sean's finger covered the trigger.

Ross raised his head as the woman came running towards them, her feet kicking up puddles of water, his hopes raised by her anguished cry.

She barrelled into Sean and, reaching out her hand, forced the rifle away.

'We don't have enough ammunition,' she hissed. 'Save it for the others.' She bent down and picked up Ross's gun, wiping it on her shirt. 'You won't need this, either,' she said, turning it in her hand. 'But maybe I'll use it on your girlfriend, eh?'

Sean laughed, then leaned forward, and with a flick of his wrist, spun the rifle around until he was holding the barrel. He stepped closer, and in one swift movement, raised it in the air and swept it down, stabbing Ross's abdomen.

Ross cried out in pain, crossed his arms across his stomach, and fell sideways, curling up into as small a target as he could manage with the wound to his leg.

Sean crouched down, leaning on the rifle, his eyes glittering. 'See, why waste bullets on a man with gut-shot?' he said. 'Why not leave the bastard to die slowly, and give him time to appreciate the fact that he should've kept his mouth shut, eh?'

He stood, then, and lashed out with his boot, catching Ross in the leg.

Ross screamed, fighting the urge to pass out.

Sean laughed before he spun on his heel and hurried back towards the truck stop, Dani trotting behind him.

Ross gulped in air, sucking the oxygen into his lungs to try and counteract the pain in his abdomen. He coughed once, then turned his head and vomited. He growled under his breath, cursing the motorcyclist with every word that came to mind, until his breathing was under control.

He wiped his mouth with the back of his hand and tried to think straight.

Dani had mentioned they were running low on ammunition, so they hadn't found the sports bag under Nina's bed.

And if they were running low on ammunition, it meant Kyle and Nina still had a chance.

He eased into a sitting position and ran his hands over his leg. Blood seeped from the wound, but slowly, despite the agony from both the original gunshot and the assault by the motorcycle rider.

He slid across the ground on his backside, until he was sitting next to the front of the vehicle, the front fender at his shoulder, and then twisted round until he could peer round the corner.

Sean and Dani were hurrying from the building towards Nina's father's pick-up truck, throwing their bags into the back of it.

Dani wrenched open the passenger door and climbed in, her short stature belying the evil that emanated from her. She slammed the door, then wound down the window and called to Sean.

He jogged over to her, and Ross watched as a heated exchange took place before Sean threw up his hands in exasperation and stalked across to one of the bowsers.

Ross's heart lurched.

He knew that the fuel company had returned and emptied the tank beneath the truck stop weeks ago, but he wondered whether they'd drained the fuel lines completely.

Or whether any residual fuel in the lines would set off a chain reaction with fumes from the empty tank.

Or whether he was sitting on a bomb that was about to go off.

He tore his jacket off, ripped out the cotton lining and tied it around the gunshot wound to his leg. Once satisfied the makeshift bandage would hold, he began to crawl away from the pick-up truck and the fuel bowsers, trying to put as much distance as he could between them.

Each time his leg dragged along the ground, he whimpered in pain, tears coursing down his cheeks, but he kept going.

He peered over his shoulder at the sound of loud cursing.

Sean was kicking the fuel bowser, swearing, and pointing at the useless trigger. In response, Dani waved her arms, pointing to the empty road.

Ross watched Sean as he threw the fuel line to the floor and ran to the open driver's door of the truck.

The engine roared to life, and the vehicle lurched onto the road, its wheels spinning until Sean eased off the accelerator, and then sped into the darkness.

Ross let his head fall back to the ground as the noise of the truck engine was lost to the night, and let the rain wash over him.

He took deep breaths, trying to manage the pain that

coursed through his leg, his whole body willing him into unconsciousness and oblivion from the agony, and then clenched his teeth and changed his focus to the open door to the truck stop.

He began to crawl again, every agonising movement accompanied by just one thought.

Nina.

EIGHTEEN

The rain lashed against Nina's skin, ice-cold darts that pierced her flesh, stinging as the motorbike sped away from the truck stop.

She choked back tears and wondered how on earth she'd forgive herself if anything happened to Ross. She silently cursed the man behind her.

FBI agent or not, he had a hell of a lot of explaining to do.

He shifted against her body, and she became aware of a breeze on her left shoulder where he'd leaned back slightly, easing the pressure on his wound.

Nina kept a wary eye on the fuel gauge, but at half-full, the huge tank showed no signs of being damaged by gunshots.

She began to shiver, her jacket and thin shirt soaked

through. Her clothes whipped against her skin in the biting wind while water puddled in her seat, drenching her jeans.

Numb, she flexed her fingers on the handlebars and then brought the machine back to a steady cruising speed.

Kyle leaned forward. 'How much further into town?'

'Another couple of miles,' she said, then frowned and changed down a gear, slowing the motorbike.

As the road straightened out, an abandoned car appeared on the horizon.

'Is that…?'

Kyle placed his hand on her shoulder. 'Stop about twenty yards before we get there.'

Nina did as she was told and brought the bike to a stop on the asphalt where he'd indicated. She lowered her feet to the ground and left it running in first gear.

They sat for a moment, staring at the vehicle in front of them.

The driver's and passenger's doors had been left open, the vehicle at a skewed angle to the road, its front fender dipping into the mud-soaked verge. Its headlights were off, and Nina realized the battery must have died.

She squinted through the rain. 'I can't see anyone.'

The bike shifted under her as Kyle dismounted awkwardly. She heard him grunt in pain as he jolted his shoulder.

He stared at the abandoned car before his gaze returned to her.

'Stay here. There's no need for you to see this.' He began to move away, then seemed to have second thoughts and looked over his shoulder. 'Keep the engine running,' he called. 'And stay sharp. They're going to be following us.'

Nina swallowed, raised her hand in reply, and focused her attention on the road behind. She swore.

'I *knew* I never should have come back.'

————

Kyle approached the car at a steady pace, his senses alert to the abandoned vehicle and the undergrowth that encroached on either side of the road.

He instinctively reached to his waistband and then cursed. Without a gun, he felt naked, exposed.

The car had been driven off the road, onto the ragged edge of the asphalt where it met the verge.

He slowed, his pace dictated by caution – and experience. He stepped across to the opposite side of the road as he drew closer, so that his silhouette wouldn't be seen in the vehicle's mirrors if Hudson's people had left a trap for him.

Beyond his position, the swollen creek roared, the water churning over the concrete bridge that had been swamped under the deluge that had drenched the valley. The crash of debris hitting the metal girders filled the air, masking any other noises around him.

His vulnerability out in the open threatened him, fighting against every training scenario and hands-on experience he'd encountered, and he fought down the urge to hurry. He had one chance at this, and he had to get it right.

Kyle spotted the edge of the flood line lapping at the road surface only metres from the vehicle and watched it for a moment, checking the water level wasn't rising any further.

The last thing he wanted was to be swept away in the vehicle, trapped under the raging torrent as it tore through the valley.

Satisfied the water level had peaked, he continued to approach the car, his breathing calm, his heartbeat solid, steadied by the adrenaline coursing through his veins.

The hiss of the rain on the asphalt masked his footsteps, and, as he walked, he thought briefly of the woman who had driven him away from danger.

He knew Ross had spoken fondly of her to John, almost putting her on a pedestal in his enthusiasm when he'd learned she'd be returning to Mistake Creek.

He wondered, briefly, what their history was. She was strong and capable, yet there was a vulnerability there he'd seen – the way she'd turned to Ross for reassurance as they'd been hiding at the truck stop.

He pushed the thought aside, ducked as he drew near the vehicle, and jogged towards it, dropping to a crouch as he drew level with the open passenger door.

A flash of lightning coursed across the night sky, illuminating the front seats, and Kyle cursed, turning his head.

He blinked to recover his night vision, the image of blood spatter across the inside of the vehicle's windshield and dashboard imprinted on his eyelids.

No stranger to death, he took a few precious seconds to gather his thoughts, to breathe, and to steel himself for the next steps he knew he'd have to take.

Once his night vision had recovered sufficiently, he reached out and pushed the door open further so he could search the vehicle. He hauled himself into the passenger seat, gritted his teeth, and checked the body of the man slumped across the steering wheel.

'Sorry, John,' he murmured as he worked through his pockets, keeping his gaze averted from his partner's unfocused staring eyes.

The dead man's clothes were soaked through from the rain that had blown through the open door in the hours that he'd lain there, and Kyle pulled out a thin fold of sodden dollar bills, tossing them to the floor. A bulge in the other pocket revealed a cigarette lighter, a familiar embossed logo stamped into the metal casing. He returned it to John's pocket, leaned back, and tried to picture what had happened.

He figured the attacker had wrenched open the driver's door and shot John at close range before he'd had a chance to react. The killing bullet had been low calibre, jerking John's body backwards, before he'd slumped onto the wheel.

A dark stain covered the head rest of the seat, and for a moment, he wondered if John had been stunned by the force of the vehicle leaving the road, or had tried to manoeuvre the vehicle while his killer had approached, knowing that he faced a cold-blooded execution.

He shook his head to clear the thought, cursed as his search through John's clothing yielded nothing further, and sat back in the passenger seat.

His head snapped up at a faint sound carrying across the noise of the wind and rain, and he leaned on the vehicle's door.

'Kyle!'

He launched his body out of the seat, then stepped onto the running board and raised himself until he was standing, leaning on the roof of the car for support, and craned his neck.

Nina was still on the motorbike, her feet planted on the ground each side of it, frantically waving to him, before looking over her shoulder.

He raised his gaze and swore.

Headlights approached from the distance, only a few miles away.

Minutes.

He squinted through the rain towards the swollen

creek. Its angry roar echoed with the thunder shaking the skies, and he punched the roof of the vehicle in frustration.

They wouldn't be able to cross it for days, even using the tough adventure bike they'd escaped on.

Nina called his name again, her voice urgent, carried away on the wind.

Kyle dropped back into the seat and began pulling at the fabric lining of the door panel, his fingernails tearing at the seams.

He cursed as a small piece of fabric fell away, leaving a hole too small for his hand. He gritted his teeth, and pulled again at the cloth, until he pulled a strip of material away. He pushed his fingers underneath, then tugged until the lining tore, and caught the gun that fell from the concealed pocket.

Tucking it into his waistband to keep his hands free, he pushed his fingers back into the lining and felt around until he found a spare magazine of ammunition, which he pocketed. Further back, he found what he was really looking for.

His fingers wrapped around the small rectangular object, and he pulled.

Gripping the satellite phone, he switched it on. He slipped out of the passenger seat and jogged round to the driver's side of the vehicle while he waited for the phone to power up.

He gently pushed John's body to one side so he could perch on the driver's seat while he worked. Tearing the fabric from the inside of the door, he slipped the more important contents into his pocket, ignoring the hidden case notes that flapped from the ruined panel, catching in the wind, and concentrated on the phone.

It was fully charged, and he breathed a sigh of relief, then cursed when he saw the signal levels.

Nothing.

He lowered himself back into the vehicle and stuffed the satellite phone into his pocket. His gaze fell to his dead partner slumped in the driver's seat. There'd be one more thing he'd have to do before he left the scene.

'I'm sorry,' he murmured. 'I wish there was another way.'

He leaned forward and pulled John's shirt from his waistband, then tore a length of fabric away. Reaching into the dead man's pockets, he felt around until his fingers clasped hold of a metallic object he'd previously left alone, and pulled.

The cigarette lighter glistened in contrast to the gloom of the vehicle, and he gritted his teeth, wishing a better end for his colleague.

'Kyle! Hurry!'

Nina's voice galvanized him into action.

He patted the dead man on the shoulder, flicked the fuel cap release in the side of the driver's door, then stepped out of the car and hurried round the side of the vehicle.

Pulling open the fuel cap, he stuffed the length of shirt

into the gaping hole, until only a fraction of the material remained. He flicked the cigarette lighter.

The flame died as quickly as it had appeared.

'Fuck!'

NINETEEN

Kyle tapped the side of the cigarette lighter on the palm of his hand and then flicked it once more.

A yellow flame shot upwards, and he jerked his head out of the way as it flared.

'Shit!'

He checked the satellite phone and gun were secure and then took a deep breath. He'd have seconds, at most.

He exhaled and thrust the cigarette lighter at the material. A momentary realisation hit him that he had no idea how much fuel was left in the tank. He held his breath until the flame caught, and then he fled.

He powered his legs along the wet asphalt, his ears straining for the familiar *crump* of the flames taking hold.

The air rushed past him as the fire devoured the oxygen in the immediate vicinity, sucking it back in the direction of the vehicle, before he was thrown forward with the force of the fire shooting out across the road.

He had a split second to turn his body to avoid landing on his injured shoulder, then grunted as his body met the surface of the road. He rolled, covering his face and neck with his jacket.

Searing heat passed over him, and he heard something metallic strike the asphalt close to where he lay, spat out by the flames.

As the noise from the initial roar of the fire died, he opened his eyes at the sound of an approaching motorbike.

The front wheel stopped inches from his nose.

'Get up!' Nina screamed. 'They're nearly here!'

He scrambled to his feet, and then used the gun to smash the front and rear lights.

'What are you doing?' yelled Nina. 'I won't be able to see.'

'We can't risk them spotting us straight away,' he said.

She held the bike steady while he threw his body into the pillion seat.

'Go!' he yelled.

Nina flicked her wrist, easing out the clutch and gently releasing the throttle, in anticipation of the surge of power from the engine beneath her.

Instead, it died.

Kyle peered round her body and stared at the dials, trying to comprehend what had happened.

'What did you do?'

'Nothing!' she shouted over her shoulder.

'Shit. Hang on.'

Nina struggled to hold the bike upright as he clambered off and fell into a crouch next to the front wheel.

'The wire's fallen out,' he said. 'Don't move your feet. It's got to be here somewhere.'

Nina planted her feet and moved her head from side to side, her eyes searching for the elusive piece of wire while Kyle held the cigarette lighter in his hand, the flame sputtering in the wind.

'Here!'

He moved sideways and held up the wire.

'Hurry,' Nina urged. She pointed over his shoulder – the headlights were bearing down on them, only a mile away, approaching the curve in the road.

Once the vehicle rounded the corner, they'd be caught in its powerful beams.

Kyle turned back to the motorbike, wrapped the wire back into its temporary housing, and then stood up as the ignition lights flickered to life.

Nina pressed the starter.

The lights flickered, and then died.

'Shit.'

Kyle bent down again, absorbed in his work.

Adrenaline surged through his body, yet his

movements were calm and measured as he twisted the wire, trying to complete the circuit.

After what seemed an age, the ignition lights shone.

Nina flexed her fingers around the throttle lever, and Kyle closed his eyes and crossed his fingers.

Please let this work.

His eyes shot open as the engine caught. He let out a triumphant shout, before climbing onto the bike and threading his arm around her waist.

'Get out of here!'

———————

Nina shook her head to clear the tears from her line of vision.

Her arms ached from steering the motorbike over the rough uneven surface of the farm track they'd been following for the past few miles, and the cold rain froze her to the bone. Her clothes were soaked, the wind chill adding to her discomfort.

She checked the mirrors again, searching for any obvious signs of a pursuit, but it appeared that her quick thinking at taking the muddy track away from the main road had paid dividends.

When she'd first made the decision to leave the main road, Kyle had cursed, demanding she turn around.

He'd fallen silent when she'd explained the track was a

fire trail, designed to run between the farming properties to offer protection should the unthinkable happen and a fire take hold.

It offered them an escape route away from their pursuers and, hopefully, to rescue.

Nina had pulled over onto the side of the track after half a mile, and they'd waited, peering through a break in the trees at the highway below as Sean and Dani had left their stolen pick-up truck and approached the burning vehicle.

An argument had ensued, and Dani had kicked the side of the pick-up truck before they'd jumped back in and turned back in the opposite direction to the creek.

'What do you think they're doing?' asked Nina.

'No time to worry about it,' Kyle had said. 'Get going.'

She sniffled, the man behind her oblivious to his surroundings now. He appeared to be exhausted, his body slumped against hers, his breath warm on her neck.

But she'd seen another side to him. The calculated way in which he'd approached the abandoned car spoke volumes about the story Ross had told her.

FBI agent.

As she guided the bike's wheels through another series of deep potholes, she ignored the pained grunt from Kyle and instead wondered what division of the FBI he worked for.

She squinted through the darkness along the unsealed

farm track ahead of her. She remembered riding along it on dirt bikes with Ross and his brother, but her ability to pick out any familiar landmarks was hindered by the lack of moonlight.

Occasional flashes of lightning helped her to gauge her surroundings as the storm retreated across the horizon. A blanket of purple and white light illuminated the sky for a few precious seconds, and Nina's attention shot to the right.

A large building appeared in the gloom, set against the undulating hillside.

A barn.

Her mind made up, she eased the throttle back, changed down a gear, and steered the bike across a narrow muddy path.

'Where the hell are you going?'

She ignored the shout from behind her, and the expletives that followed it, and instead concentrated on threading the motorbike along the ruts and furrows that cut through the track.

Nina ducked as a thin, low-hanging branch swung into view at the last minute, Kyle cursing behind her when he copied her a second too late as she wove the bike through the debris covering their path.

Up ahead, she could see a large silhouette looming above them, blocking out the lightning that still coursed through the sky behind it.

The track leveled out, and she throttled up, eager to reach her destination.

The barn looked more decrepit than it had when she was a teenager, but the roof looked intact, and the walls were solid enough.

'Get the door,' she called over her shoulder as she brought the bike to a standstill.

She ignored the cursing from her passenger as Kyle crawled from the seat and made his way towards the building.

She squinted through the rain as he approached the barn, a moment of panic surging through her as she wondered if Ross's father now kept it locked.

She exhaled as Kyle pushed the door open wide enough to get the motorbike through and drove forward, ignoring his glare as she passed him and entered the wide empty space.

The dirt floor was dry under the wheels, and she relaxed a little. Turning the bike so that they could leave quickly if they needed to, she slipped the gears into neutral and killed the engine.

An ancient aroma of disused rusting machinery, neglected and worn, filled the dark space. Dust filled the air, and Nina coughed as the spores began to seep into her lungs.

Kyle slammed the door shut, pulled a wooden beam across to act as a lock, and then peered through the gap in the boards. Once satisfied they hadn't been followed, he swung round to face her and pulled out the flashlight from under his jacket. He angled the beam to the floor so as not to blind her. 'Why the hell have we stopped?'

Nina ignored the remark, removed her helmet, and began to wring out her wet hair. She flicked her hands to lose the moisture and tried to fight down the tightness that was beginning to manifest in her lungs.

'I asked you a question,' said Kyle, and moved in front of her, glowering.

Nina took a step back at the look in his eyes, his fury boring into her. 'I'm exhausted,' she said. 'I need a moment to get my breath back.' She held her hands up. 'Just give me a minute.'

His jaw clenched, frustration oozing from every pore, but she stared at him, waiting for his acceptance. 'Okay. Ten minutes, no more,' he said, and spun on his heel.

Nina sighed with relief, her lungs rattling. Her breathing was worsening, the dust and grain spores in the building adding to her discomfort.

She'd been struggling since she'd returned to the valley days ago, the mountain range acting as a trap for the smog and pollutants in the air. With no rain to clear the atmosphere until that afternoon, the air had become static, slowly breaking down her resistance.

Now, she berated herself for not carrying her inhaler as she had when she was a teenager.

She bit back tears that threatened to fall. Sheer frustration filled her, the thought that if she'd remained on the coast, she wouldn't have trouble breathing, the cleaner sea air a respite from her childhood health issues.

And the fact that she wouldn't have become involved in whatever was going on in Mistake Creek, and maybe – just maybe – Ross would still be okay.

She leaned forward as the tightness took over her chest and tried to call out to Kyle as she doubled over, wheezing.

TWENTY

'Nina, what's wrong? What's happening?'

Kyle dashed forward and put his arm around her shoulder.

Within seconds, her demeanour had changed from temperamental to one of panic, her breathing laboured. Her eyes were wide, frightened, as he leaned down to her.

'Is it an asthma attack?'

She nodded mutely and held her hand up to him.

He let her concentrate on her breathing, but it seemed a fruitless exercise. Her face was turning pale, and she was beginning to shake.

'Where's your inhaler?' he demanded. 'I'll get it for you.'

'Truck stop,' she gasped.

He swallowed, the reality of the situation hitting him

hard. He had never had to deal with an asthma attack, but he knew they could be fatal. He kept his face and voice calm, not wishing to alarm the woman in front of him.

'Here,' he said, coaxing her into a sitting position. 'Don't panic. I'm here.'

His words belied his own emotions. He had no idea what to do. His mind worked overtime, trying to remember anything he'd read or learned about asthma attacks. They could kill, he knew, depending on the person's frailty and the state of their lungs.

He thought of the damp air Nina had been subjected to for the past two hours, the physical exertion she'd endured, and cursed the dust and mildew that peppered the air in the barn they were now sheltering in.

He waited until Nina had sat on the floor and then joined her, wrapping his arms around her and pulling her close, trying to keep her warm.

Her lungs rattled with the effort of seeking oxygen, and Kyle fought down his own panic, instead conjuring up words to soothe her, hoping that his voice would keep her calm so that the attack didn't worsen.

The phrases seemed alien to him, removed from his usual tendency to bark orders or respond in monosyllables.

He closed his eyes and listened to Nina breathing, and he tried to recall the last time he'd been this close to someone. The shock hit him hard as he realized it had been more than a year.

He shuffled around her until he could see her face, and waited until her gaze found his. 'I'm not going anywhere. It'll be okay.'

His mind spun. He had no idea how long an asthma attack could last – or whether this one would be fatal. He could see that Nina was trying her hardest not to panic, but her breathing was becoming shallower by the minute.

He couldn't imagine the terror she must be feeling.

His emotions ran from frustration at the time he was losing, to the thought that the feisty woman he'd met at the truck stop who had helped him escape could be so weakened by her lungs fighting for air.

He swallowed, remembering his promise to Ross that he'd keep her safe, and wondered how on earth he was going to complete his mission and keep his word.

She slumped in his arms, and Kyle shifted his body, gently lifting Nina's head so it rested in his lap. He smoothed her hair away from her face, then leaned over and pulled his jacket across the floor before dragging it over her shoulders.

He reached underneath until his hand was between her shoulder blades and began to rub her back, trying to reassure her.

As her ragged breaths shook her body, her fingers wrapped round his other hand, taking him by surprise.

At that moment, he wondered if Nina and Ross had any feelings between them, and regret shook his core. He was so damn tired of being alone.

'It's okay, Nina. Just breathe,' he murmured. 'I've got you.'

———

Nina tried to fight down the panic that threatened to engulf her.

She had a vague sense of Kyle talking to her, his voice different, tender, and the words soothed her.

She reached inside her shirt, rubbing her sternum with her fingertips. She was never sure if the motion worked, but it had been something her mother had always done when she was a child, and the familiarity comforted her.

She wondered how bad the attack would be, and how long it would last. Closing her eyes, she concentrated on squeezing the air into her lungs.

Strong arms wrapped around her and pulled her close, Kyle's words washing over her.

She wiped at her eyes, fighting down the urge to cry, the despair of leaving Ross behind too much to bear. Crying would make breathing more difficult, and she forced the thought away, instead trying to convince herself that he'd be okay, that somehow he'd survive, that someone would find him and help him.

She couldn't remember ever feeling so tired, so exhausted.

She cursed her own stupidity for not doing as Ross had told her, for not putting her inhaler in her pocket, and then

before she could think anything else, her breathing began
to settle, and she closed her eyes, exhausted.

TWENTY-ONE

Jock Hudson grappled with the door of the farmhouse as a powerful gust of wind whipped the handle from his grip, sending the door slamming into the wall of the passageway.

Stepping over the threshold, his overcoat shedding rivulets of water onto the tiled floor, he pushed the door shut and leaned against it, his breathing laboured.

Forty years of smoking cheap cigarettes were beginning to take their toll – not that he'd ever tell anyone. The added effect of exposure to depleted uranium while serving in the Gulf all those years ago exacerbated the problem. Or so his doctor had told him.

Truth was, they didn't know whether it was the uranium or the cigarettes that caused the cancer.

All he did know was that it was inoperable, especially

as his medical coverage was non-existent, and the army sure as hell wasn't going to help him now.

He set his jaw.

He wouldn't give up yet, though. First, he had business to take care of, before he dealt with the ugly truth that was death.

Now it was time for the American government to pay for what they'd done to him.

He removed his coat, shook the worst of the water from it, and hung it on a hook near the door, placing his hat above it. He ran his hand through his hair as he moved along the passageway towards the kitchen and the sound of voices.

As he entered the room, the words fell silent, and six expectant faces turned towards him.

He stalked over to the sink, filled a glass with water, and gulped the contents. He wiped his mouth across his sleeve, then swung round and launched the empty glass at the wall next to the table.

It exploded against the plasterwork, shards raining through the air.

The six men at the table raised their arms to cover their faces, the older two grim, while the younger four members of the group tried to hide their fright at the sudden outburst.

Jock's heavy breathing filled the shocked silence, a thick rasping sound that did little to disguise his fury.

'Look at me,' he commanded.

One by one, the men twisted in their seats, brushing slivers of glass from their hair and shoulders and forcing themselves to face their leader's anger.

'Now,' he said, a steely expression in his eyes. 'Tell me about the fuck-up here. Who the hell betrayed me?'

A nervous cough came from the end of the table. An acne-scarred man in his late twenties leaned forward.

'John Asher and Kyle Roberts,' he said. 'Turns out they were FBI agents.'

Hudson paced the floor. 'Why didn't their backgrounds show up when you checked the first time around?'

Sweat broke out across the younger man's forehead, his eyes darting to the men sitting on either side of him. Almost as one, they leaned back in their chairs, as if to distance themselves from the confrontation.

'They must've been deep cover, sir. Nothing showed up until today – and we're using the latest systems.'

Hudson waved his hand. 'Excuses,' he spat. 'What happened out there?'

'Kyle tried to overpower the driver, who luckily had the sense to carry a knife in the cab,' said an older man, his face solemn. 'The driver managed to stab Kyle before he escaped.'

'And John?' Hudson folded his arms across his chest and stood at the head of the table, his feet apart. 'What happened there?'

'We think he saw Kyle fall out of the cab – Sean and Dani were closest to him. Apparently, he took one look at what was happening next to the truck, then stole a car, collected Roberts, and tried to escape to Mistake Creek. Roberts jumped out at the top of the ridge.'

'Did John make it?'

The man shook his head. 'No – Sean and Dani caught up with him. The creek's flooded, so he couldn't get across. They found him in the vehicle on the main road. She said it was like shooting fish in a barrel.'

Hudson pursed his lips. Dani was a liability sometimes, but an effective killer. He hoped he never found himself on the wrong side of her temper.

'Where are Sean and Dani now?'

The younger man spoke up. 'We lost contact with them after that,' he said. 'The storm threw our communications system offline – there's just too much static.'

A large man, African American, moved from where he had appeared at the doorway to the kitchen and kicked the shards of glass to one side. 'Maybe they're sheltering somewhere,' he suggested, his voice low and calm. 'It'd be pretty hard to ride a motorbike in this weather.'

Hudson nodded. 'True. No sense in worrying about them at the moment. They're more than capable of looking out for themselves.'

'What about the truck, sir? Have you heard anything from the driver?'

Hudson's gaze flicked to the man who had spoken. One of the younger members of the rag-tag group of mercenaries Hudson had ensnared, the man's forearms bore the tell-tale pinpricks of a habitual drug user. The youth's eyes were glossy, and Hudson wondered how the hell he'd ended up with so many loose ends to tidy away before his mission would be complete.

'Sir?' One of the other men spoke, breaking Hudson's reverie.

Only then did Hudson allow a small smile to reach his mouth, his frustration about Kyle Roberts temporarily stayed. 'The truck made it through before the landslide,' he said.

The room filled with the sound of clapping. The six men pushed back their chairs and stood to congratulate him, slapping him on the back and turning to each other to share their excitement.

One of the other men leaned forward in his seat. 'What do we do next, sir?'

'We continue to activate phase two of the plan,' said Hudson. He checked his watch. 'That means you've got less than five hours to grab what you need, clean this place out, and be ready to roll.' He looked each man in the eye, his gaze roaming round the table. 'If you're not ready, the rest of us won't wait. Understood?'

'Sir, yes, sir!'

The men jumped to their feet and saluted.

'Dismissed.'

Hudson stood back as the men filed past him, then held out his hand to stop the youngest.

The man's eyes widened, and his Adam's apple bobbed in his throat. 'Sir?'

'Get that communications system up and running, soldier. I want to know *exactly* where that truck is.'

'Yes, sir.'

Hudson watched him go, then his attention snapped back to the large man standing at the door. 'What do you think, Larry?'

'I think we need to stick to the plan,' the man said. 'Keep the men calm, make sure they don't panic. Get the job done.'

TWENTY-TWO

Nina coughed once before her eyelids shot open.

She was lying on her father's old jacket, the lining stained with blood. She tried to remember where she was, and then recalled the escape from the truck stop on the motorbike, the abandoned car with Kyle's dead partner inside, and finding the old barn to hide in.

She raised her head, waited for the bout of dizziness to subside, then eased into a sitting position.

Her chest ached, her lungs on fire from the attack that had wracked her body, the cold air sending chills up her arms. She frowned.

Kyle was nowhere to be seen.

Nor was the motorbike.

She cursed under her breath before a low grunt reached her ears. She hauled herself to her feet using the wall for support and saw Kyle leaning against the motorbike on the other side of the barn.

She began to walk towards him, a little unsteadily at first, before she regained her balance. The old boards creaked under her weight, and Kyle's head jerked round, his eyes blazing. Anger surged through her.

'What are you doing? Were you thinking of leaving without me?'

'You're tired. Exhausted. I was trying to see if I could ride the bike.'

'You mean you *were* going to leave.'

'Not without you.'

Nina folded her arms across her chest. 'I don't believe you.'

'I don't care what you think.'

He turned back to the machine, flexing his fingers on the handlebars, and began to push it towards the locked barn doors.

'You're bleeding again.'

He stopped, and his shoulders slumped. 'I thought I might be.'

Nina hurried to where he stood, leaned over the motorbike, and pushed his hands out of the way, before kicking the stand out and leaning the machine on it.

'Stop. Let me take a look.'

She led the way back to where the old jacket lay on the floor, and then waited for Kyle to join her.

When he lifted his arms to peel off his t-shirt, she

swallowed then pointed at the floor. 'Sit down there. Hold the flashlight so I can see what I'm doing.'

Once Kyle had settled, Nina knelt beside him.

'Sorry if this hurts.'

She peeled back the blood-soaked bandage and checked her watch.

It had only been six hours since she and Ross had applied their rough first aid to the FBI agent.

She sniffled. It felt like a lifetime ago.

'What does it look like?'

Kyle twisted his neck to try and see what she was doing, but Nina placed her hand on his cheek and pushed back.

'Stop moving. If you can't keep still, I can't do this.'

He sighed, an impatient exhalation of air that held undertones of a curse, but kept still while she worked, emitting only a grunt when she peeled back the rest of the stained fabric.

'Sorry.'

Nina sat back on her heels, the bloodied material in one hand, her other hand on Kyle's shoulder. She stared at the wound.

Although the bleeding had now stopped, the motion of pushing the motorcycle across the barn had forced open any skin that had attempted to heal. It was obvious that he'd have to get medical attention or risk getting an infection.

'How bad is it?'

'Um, it's...'

'Don't bullshit me. I can feel it, remember?'

'Okay,' said Nina. 'You can't ride the bike. You have to stay pillion.'

His head twitched slightly, and he looked at her out the corner of his eye. 'We can't risk you having another asthma attack.'

Nina lowered her hand from his shoulder as he turned to face her. She swallowed. 'I-I'll be fine,' she said. 'I'm usually okay for a few hours after an attack. We can patch up your shoulder again using the lining from that other old jacket you were wearing. It's the best I can do.'

She gazed around the barn. 'I can't see anything cleaner we could use.' Her eyes fell back to Kyle.

He hadn't moved. Instead, he was watching her intently, a kink at the corner of his mouth.

'What?' Nina stared back. 'What did I say?'

He raised himself into a kneeling position. 'Nothing. You scared the shit out of me earlier.'

'What, my asthma attack? Sorry – I forgot my inhaler.'

'Stop apologising.'

His eyes bored into hers, and for the first time, she noticed how green flecks appeared in his blue irises, lending his usual cold demeanour a flash of concern.

'Right,' she said, standing. 'Stay there. Don't move. I'll get that jacket.'

When she returned, she concentrated on cleaning his arm, keeping the conversation business-like. 'You haven't told me what's going on,' she said, 'Such as, why is the FBI in Mistake Creek?'

'We got a tip-off that Ross's neighbours might be dealing drugs in large quantities,' he said, and pulled his t-shirt back on, careful to lift it over the makeshift bandage.

'Why is Ross involved?'

'He was the one who told us.'

'Oh.'

Nina moved towards an old moth-eaten armchair that had been dumped in one corner and perched on the arm.

'What made you think they're drug dealers?'

Kyle stood, then leaned against the wall and peered between the cracks in the wood.

'Ross told us the property had been sold three years ago to a guy from the city. He didn't go out of his way to make friends in the area and seemed to keep to himself,' he said. 'Then, about a year ago, Ross noticed some strange activities – trucks arriving late in the night, crops being stripped from around the house with no replacement sowing activities, that sort of thing.'

Nina choked out a laugh. 'You're kidding, right? Ross told me all Hudson grew there was cattle feed and pistachios. The only thing people get irate about round here is when their neighbours outbid them on water irrigation rights. Are you sure this isn't what this is all about? Retaliation?'

Kyle shook his head. 'As soon as he arrived three years ago, he harvested the old crops then replanted the whole lot with castor oil plants. But it's what's going on in the outbuildings that had Ross concerned. He was convinced that their neighbour was using the property as a drug laboratory.'

'And was he?'

Kyle shrugged and moved away from the door. 'Sort of. I went in three months ago undercover. It took me three months before that to build up their trust. When Ross contacted us, we'd had Hudson on the radar about possible drug offences for a while, but it wasn't until the first of us went in undercover that we found out how big his operation really was.'

Nina crossed the floor. 'You bastard. You should've told me this earlier – we could have done something before Phil got killed!' Anger surged through her. 'Why the *hell* didn't you stop them before it went this far?'

'We were meant to, don't you get it? That's why we were there.'

'What went wrong?'

'They sprung it on us this morning. We spent most of today loading the truck with the goods,' he said. 'I was supposed to stop it – I was there, next to the driver, ready to go with him.' He paused, and Nina saw pure fury cross his face.

'What happened?'

Kyle flexed his arm, testing his injured shoulder. 'I realized something had gone wrong when I got into the cab with the driver,' he said. 'It was just a feeling – you do this long enough, you learn to trust your instincts. I realized I had one last chance to try to stop them, so I tried to overpower the driver. I thought if I could steal the truck, I could ruin Hudson's plans. I didn't expect the driver to have a knife.'

Nina stared at him, open-mouthed. 'What did you do?'

'I managed to turn, just in time. He caught me off-guard,' he said, looking at his hands. 'I should've expected something like that, but I was just so wrapped up in thinking through how I was going to get the truck away from the farm and somewhere safe.'

Nina noted the tinge of regret in his voice and stepped closer. 'You're lucky to be alive,' she said. 'He could've killed you – look what he did to your partner.'

Kyle nodded. 'John saw what happened and stole a car so we could get away from Hudson's place. We decided to split up. John was going to try to get to the town and raise the alarm there. I figured I could follow the ridge line as cover and get to Ross's farm, but they came after me in two pick-up trucks.'

'Where's the truck now?'

'It's heading for the city.'

'What?'

'You see? I need to get somewhere I can use this satellite phone, Nina. *Fast*. I have to warn the office that truck is heading towards them before it reaches its destination and the shipment is split up and distributed. I'm the only one who knows.'

Nina wiped her eyes, took a deep breath, and put her hands on her hips.

'I can help you,' she said. 'I'll drive the motorbike, and I'll get you to a phone.'

Kyle opened his mouth to reply, but she held a hand up, silencing him.

'In return, as soon as you make that call, we go back to the truck stop and find Ross.'

He frowned and then nodded. 'Okay. Deal.'

He held out his hand.

Nina shook it, then loosened her grip, pulled the old jacket around her shoulders, and strode towards the motorbike.

'Right. Let's go.'

TWENTY-THREE

Nina swore under her breath as the heavy machine slid across the track from under her for what seemed the hundredth time since they'd left the safety of the barn.

Although she'd agreed with Kyle that they would head towards the suspect's property, questions were still running through her mind as she pulled hard on the handlebars to correct the motorbike's balance.

She bit her lip and became more conscious of Kyle's weight behind her, his chest pressing against her spine.

He'd moved his head away from hers after the bike had hit the first pothole, sending her skull jerking backwards and making contact with his jaw.

He'd cursed, loudly, before adjusting his position.

She pushed the left handlebar away from her and steered the bike safely through the large puddle that covered the width of the track.

Kyle's body moved against her, and he shouted in her ear over the noise of the engine.

'Can't you go any faster?'

'No!' she yelled. 'Not unless you want to end up in a ditch underneath this thing!'

He fell silent, letting her concentrate on the narrow track that disappeared ahead of them into the night.

Nina had been tempted to open the throttle, to hurry towards their destination when they'd first left the barn, but within seconds realized it wasn't possible.

The surface of the track was deteriorating by the minute, the water run-off from the ridge above tearing away stones and gravel as it passed.

She swerved to avoid another falling branch, straightened the bike, and eased it round a bend.

'Change of plan,' shouted Kyle. 'Head for Ross's property instead.'

'Why?'

'It's closer. We can borrow a vehicle from there. It'll be faster than this.'

She nodded.

His suggestion was timely. Although she reckoned they'd only been traveling for twenty minutes, her arms were already sore, the muscles in her shoulder sockets painful.

'Stop before we reach the entrance.'

'Okay.'

Another flash of lightning illuminated the landscape,

and seeing the outline of the signpost depicting the start of the Flanagan property, Nina swung the bike over to the left.

The wheels bucked as she rode it across a small fallen branch and other debris before braking and switching off the engine.

She waited until Kyle had dismounted, then swung her leg over the seat. Her legs buckled as her feet touched the ground.

Kyle's arm wrapped around her waist, his injured shoulder knocking against her as he reached out his other hand to help her steady the bike.

'You're exhausted,' he said.

'I'll be fine. What do we do with this?'

'We'll pull it into the trees here,' he said. 'Out of sight. We might need it again.'

They pushed the motorbike between two large trees, pulled branches over its metalwork, and looped their helmets over the handlebars.

Kyle stood on the road, inspected the hiding place, then nodded, satisfied.

'What's your plan?' Nina asked, slicking her wet hair out of her eyes. 'Why stop here?'

'The original owners of that bike didn't end up at your truck stop by accident. They were looking for me. My cover got blown. Now they'll be looking for the bike, and I don't want to put Ross's family in danger.' He peered over his shoulder at the rough track that led away up the hill towards the Flanagan property. 'I want to phone my superiors before I go any further. I need to warn them about that truck heading their way.'

'And then?'

'Then I get them to send reinforcements so I can meet them at a rendezvous point.' He squinted up at the sky through the rain. 'The lightning storm's passing. They should be able to get a helicopter here in this.'

Nina sniffed and tried to disguise the shiver that rocked her body. 'OK, well, let's go.'

'Wait.'

He held out his arm to stop her. 'You need to understand how dangerous this is. Stay behind me at all times, and do what I tell you. We don't know where Sean and Dani are. No running off, okay?'

'I understand.'

'Can you run, or will that set off your asthma?'

'I'll be fine. I can run a bit.'

'Good. Come on.'

He began to jog towards the property, leading the way along the muddy track and then over the iron cattle-grid that formed a boundary between the public road and the property.

Nina followed behind him, grateful for the exercise as warmth began to return to her numb limbs. The track leading to the property was undulating and slippery, and her boots seemed heavier with each step as she tried to keep up with the FBI agent. Twice she nearly lost her footing.

The second time, Kyle heard her gasp and shot out his hand to steady her. After that, he slowed to a fast walk.

'No sense breaking our necks before we get there,' he explained.

As they drew near the crest of the hill, he pulled her to the side of the track and pushed her into a crouching position before moving forward.

The highest part of the track allowed them a panoramic view of the property that lay cradled in the small valley created between the hill and the ridge that rose above it in the darkness.

Lights blazed from the property and the surrounding outbuildings, illuminating the expansive yard and the vehicles scattered around it.

'Shit.'

'What?'

'We're too late.'

'What do you mean?' Nina fought down the panic rising in her chest. 'What's going on?'

Kyle squeezed her hand. 'I was afraid this might have happened,' he said. 'I think Ross's father and brother have been taken hostage.'

'Why?'

Kyle moved his hand across her face at her anguished cry. 'Keep your voice down!' he snapped.

Nina took a step back at the sharpness of his voice. She

watched his shoulders heave as he fought to calm down before he lowered his hand. She spoke before he had a chance to try and apologize.

'What makes you think they've been taken?'

'When was the last time you knew of a farmer leaving all his lights on at night?'

Nina let her gaze wander over the property below. Kyle was right. Electricity was expensive. Maybe Ross's father would leave a house light on, above the front door, in case of a late-night visitor, but all the lights on the outbuildings as well?

Never.

'What do we do?' she asked when he didn't respond.

Kyle was watching her, almost assessing her.

'What?'

A rueful smile creased his mouth. 'Right now, most people I've known would have turned tail and run in the other direction.'

'They're like family to me, Kyle.' She put her hands on her hips. 'So, what do we do now?'

He sighed and returned his gaze to the farmstead below. Nina watched as his eyes flickered and realized he was planning something, discarding ideas, and then settling on a way forward. She bit her lip and waited, too anxious to interrupt.

'Okay,' he said finally. 'We're going to get ourselves into position behind that white four-wheel drive parked over on the left. You can stay there while I recce the area, see if I can find out what's been going on here.'

Without waiting for her response, he took her hand and began to lead her down the slope towards the farmstead.

As they drew closer, he dropped into a crouch.

Nina copied him, her heart hammering. She breathed slowly and concentrated on what he wanted her to do, fighting down the fear that rose inside her.

He peered over his shoulder at her and signalled towards their target with his hands. On his count of three, they ran from their hiding place and dropped into position behind the four-wheel drive vehicle.

'Okay?' he whispered.

'Yes.'

'Stay here. I'm going to find a vehicle for us.'

Nina opened her mouth to protest, but Kyle had already crawled to the end of the four-wheel drive.

She exhaled, waited until he had disappeared, and then slid along until she could peer around the fender.

She watched as Kyle kept his body low and moved across the muddy ground until he reached another vehicle, an ancient sedan that had been in Ross's family since Nina was a teenager.

He crept along the side of the car, out of sight from the farmhouse, and then disappeared from view.

After realising he wasn't going to return straight away, Nina crept back to her original position and squatted on her heels. The rain had eased from torrential to a steady drizzle, and she rubbed her arms to try and stop the shivering that was threatening to engulf her body.

She jumped at a noise behind her, ready to scream, before Kyle dropped into a crouch next to her, a frown creasing his forehead.

'What's wrong?'

'Most of the tires have been slashed or shot out,' he murmured. 'And the front door is wide open.' His gaze met hers. 'I'm sorry, Nina. It doesn't look good.'

TWENTY-FOUR

'What are we going to do now?'

The thought that Jeff and Tim might be trussed up and held hostage in their own home turned Nina's despair to anger.

She clutched Kyle's arm. 'We have to do something.'

'We can't,' he said. 'Not yet.'

'Why?'

His jaw clenched. 'Because at the moment, no-one knows where we are,' he explained. 'We need to use that to our advantage.' He pulled the satellite phone from his pocket and held it up. 'Shit. Nothing.'

He stretched until he could peer through the windows of the vehicle. 'Maybe Ross's father has a working phone I can use,' he said, crouching back down. 'Hopefully it hasn't been found.'

'What are you going to do?'

Kyle pulled back his sleeve and checked his watch. 'I'm going to get into the house. See what's happening. And, with any luck, make that phone call.'

He reached into his waistband, extracted the gun, and checked the magazine. He punched it back into the weapon with the heel of his hand, then reached out and placed a hand on Nina's shoulder.

'Whatever you do, stay here out of sight,' he said. 'Do you understand?'

'Yes.'

'I'll come back, okay?'

'What if something happens to you?'

His mouth twitched. 'Trust me. I've done this before.'

He gave her shoulder a squeeze, then, without another word, crawled to the end of the vehicle.

Nina followed, waited until he ran towards the next vehicle, using it to mask his approach to the house, then slid into a squat and peered above the hood to monitor his progress.

As he moved across the slippery terrain towards his target, she shivered. His movements were so lithe, so precise, that she wondered what it would be like to have him in pursuit, rather than helping her.

She shook the thought from her mind and hunkered down against the side of the vehicle to wait.

———

Kyle raised his head above the four-door sedan and checked the outer layout of the farmhouse.

Before he was ready to enter the building, he wanted to make sure nothing had changed since his brief recce.

Everything depended on him now. If he failed to make the phone call, thousands of people would die, and the rest of the country would descend into panic and chaos.

Adrenaline swarmed though his veins, driving him forwards to seek out the next structure he could use as a shield.

When he'd checked the gun, it contained a full magazine of rounds. John had always insisted on concealing a weapon in the vehicle for emergencies, but neither of them had expected their well-laid plans to unravel so quickly.

In his haste to return to the motorbike after Nina had yelled out her warning of their pursuers closing in on them, Kyle hadn't had time to reach for the extra ammunition they'd hidden under the seats of the vehicle.

He swore under his breath.

Having Nina tag along was both a curse and a blessing. In one sense, he wouldn't have got this far without her, certainly not riding the motorbike with his injured shoulder.

On the other, she clouded his thoughts. Every decision he made tonight would impact upon her.

He wasn't used to having to worry about someone else. He and John had worked together for two years, almost psychic in their ability to segue their movements and decisions on a mission.

Instead, he worried. He'd begun to second-guess his own decisions. Such as leaving her behind the four-wheel drive vehicle, hoping she'd be safe while he tried to reach the damn telephone.

On previous missions, there had been collateral damage – the name the Bureau gave civilians who got in the way of the success of eliminating threats to the country. Innocent people who had been caught in the line of fire, simply in the wrong place at the wrong time. He overcame any guilt or regret by rationalising those losses against the people he'd saved by the decisions he'd made.

It was the only way he knew how to stop the guilt from spiralling out of control.

Now, he battled an overwhelming sense of longing. Everything Nina had done since leaving the truck stop was to try to help Ross and his family.

She was braver than any woman he'd met before tonight, and he'd do anything to protect her.

Kyle exhaled, concentrated on slowing his heart rate, then scuttled across to the next vehicle, a horse float that had been unhitched and abandoned in the yard, its wheels chocked by bricks.

A horse whinnied nearby, and he cursed, hoping the animal wouldn't be spooked by his presence. He tried to recall how far the paddock was from the house but in the darkness, it was impossible to gauge the distance.

Instead, he crouched and peered under the trailer, across the remaining space between himself and the building.

To the left, the front door stood wide open, the internal lights blazing out into the night. From his position, his view was restricted to the wall of the hallway, the door opening away from him.

He raised his chin and turned his attention to the other side of the doorway. With the porch in shadow, the powerful overhead lights blinding him, he couldn't tell if anyone was lying in wait, or whether the house had been abandoned.

He stood, then crept along the length of the horse float and peered around the corner.

Silence engulfed the property, the rain reduced to a steady downpour, remnants of the lightning storm rumbling every few minutes in the distance.

During his previous recce, he'd checked all the windows around the ground floor of the house, but they'd been locked shut. The only way into the house was in front of him.

Kyle released the safety on the gun and hurried forward in a stooped run, keeping his profile as low as possible.

He reached the steps leading up to the porch and tiptoed up them, diving into the cover of the shadows next to the front door, and waited.

As soon as he was sure it was safe, he pivoted on his

toes and swung the gun in a two-handed grip towards the front door, stepping into the hallway.

Starting with the ground floor, he checked each room, his senses alert for movement.

Once satisfied the downstairs area held no surprises, he moved up the staircase from the hallway and entered each of the bedrooms, then the two bathrooms.

As he stood in the last bedroom and flicked the safety switch on the gun, he finally allowed himself a moment to relax, the relief tinged with anguish that there was no sign of Ross's father or brother.

The house was empty.

With the gun still in his grip, he edged back downstairs, then rounded a corner and strode along the hallway, pushed open a door, and stepped into the room.

He reached out to his right, his fingers moving up and down the wall until he located the light switch, and flicked it.

A single bulb in the centre of the ceiling illuminated the room, its glare softened by a shade that created shadows in the corners and a pool of light above a patterned rug.

On the far side of the room, a large painting that had once depicted horses galloping on a racetrack had been ripped from the wall and thrown onto the floor. As Kyle drew closer, the tale-tell rip from a heavy boot was evident in the centre of the canvas.

A wall safe had been exposed, its door open and

documents strewn across the carpet, crackling under Kyle's boots as he pivoted, surveying the damage.

The farm's paperwork lay strewn across an old mahogany desk – invoices, delivery dockets, and scribbled notes. The computer and screen had been destroyed, and Kyle carefully sifted through the glass-strewn desk for any clues as to the family's whereabouts.

Nothing.

Kyle checked to see if his satellite phone worked. The screen remained blank, save for a system error message that confirmed his suspicions.

He swore and turned his attention to the desk phone, his hand hovering over it for a moment before he snatched it from its cradle and put it to his ear.

The single tone of a dead line cut through the static, confirming the landline had been severed – either by the storm or by those who had taken Ross's family.

He grasped the cable between his fingers, tracking its path around the edge of the room until he found the junction box, and then cursed.

The wire had been cut, rendering the landline useless.

He wracked his memory. When they'd first met, Ross had told him about a UHF radio they kept for emergencies.

He began to pull out the desk drawers, going through them one by one, but by the last drawer, he realized he was pursuing a fruitless task. The office had been thoroughly ransacked.

Instead, he hurried out of the room, down the hallway,

and out the front door and ran from vehicle to vehicle until he found Nina, cold and shivering, exactly where he'd left her. She brandished a length of wood, gripping it in her hands and ready to strike.

Her eyes opened wide at his presence before her shoulders relaxed. 'It's you,' she said, a note of relief in her voice. 'I thought they'd found me.'

'Come with me,' said Kyle. 'I need your help.'

———

Nina gasped when she saw the damage to the farm office.

She moved towards the open safe, sifting through the debris, her eyes welling up.

'They've stolen all of his mother's jewelery,' she said, wiping angrily at her tears. She inspected the wreckage strewn around the room. 'Why would they do this? Why would they take them?'

'Because they're professionals,' said Kyle.

'What do we do?'

He held up the satellite phone. 'This isn't working, and the landline's out. Ross mentioned to John in the past that they have a UHF radio here for emergencies.' He stepped closer to her. 'Do you know where they might keep it?'

She frowned, her mind working. 'I would have thought it'd be in here somewhere.'

'No,' he said. 'Drawers have been tipped out. If they'd found it here, they'd have destroyed it and tossed it.'

'How do you know?'

'It's what I would have done.' He sighed. 'I'm used to being the one that does this to people, Nina. I'm not a farmer. So, where else would Ross's family keep a radio for emergencies?'

She closed her eyes, running the layout of the house through her mind, discarding rooms as her memory worked.

'Hurry, Nina. We're running out of time.'

She opened her eyes and bit her lip. 'Try the mud room out the back.'

He followed her from the room, down the hallway towards the kitchen. 'Why there?'

She shrugged. 'It's just a guess. If there was an accident outside, they'd want help fast. No sense in having a phone in the office or somewhere else if you've got to run the length of the house to get to it.' She led the way through the kitchen to what appeared to be a closet door. 'You'd keep it somewhere everyone had access to it.'

She pushed open the door and stood aside to let Kyle pass.

The room held a musty aroma of sweat, old grass, and Jeff's favourite tobacco.

A hundred memories flooded Nina's thoughts as she stood in the middle of the room, her hands on her hips as she assessed the subtle changes that had taken place since she'd last been at the Flanagan property.

'Nina?'

The urgency in Kyle's voice galvanized her into action. Pulling open the door to a small cupboard to the right of the back door, she reached up and grabbed hold of the UHF radio set.

'How did you guess?' asked Kyle, taking the unit from her and placing it on the counter.

Nina smiled. 'The cupboard was the only thing that was different from when I was last here,' she said.

His eyebrows shot upwards before he reached into the cupboard again, a grin on his face.

'Now that's a bonus,' he said, holding up a small pistol and checking its magazine. 'Full, too,' he added, tucking it into his waistband.

'They must've surprised Jeff before he had a chance to defend himself,' said Nina.

'Maybe.' Kyle began flicking switches on the radio unit and then held up his hand before speaking. 'Stay quiet,' he said. 'I'm going to have one chance at this. I don't know who could be listening in, and I need my office to mobilize as soon as they get this written down, okay?'

Nina nodded, listening as Kyle flicked to a frequency and issued his call sign.

He waited for a few seconds, and then when there was no response, moved to the next frequency and repeated the exercise.

Nina began to pace the floor, her heart racing as the seconds become minutes and still no response issued through the radio.

The hiss of white noise as Kyle twisted the dial after each attempt began to grate on her nerves. Irritated, she resisted the urge to snatch the microphone from his grip and issue her own plea for help.

Kyle noticed her agitation and put a finger to his lips, shaking his head as he turned the dial, paused to take a breath, and then recited the call sign Nina now knew by heart.

They both surged closer to the radio unit as a voice replied almost as soon as Kyle finished speaking.

It was another man, his deep tones failing to disguise his excitement, despite the static that broke up his words.

'Good to hear from you. Where have you been?'

'On vacation,' said Kyle. 'And my phone credit ran out.'

Nina frowned before she realized both men were talking in a form of code in an attempt to confuse any eavesdroppers.

'What's the weather like?'

'Shitty. And you've got a tornado heading your way.'

A moment's silence passed before the man responded.

'Repeat that?'

'Tornado. Heading your way. Left here eight hours ago.'

'Destination?'

'As we suspected.'

Nina heard movement in the background, chairs being pushed back and a murmur of urgent voices.

'Copy that,' said the voice.

'Out,' said Kyle, and replaced the microphone. He checked his watch. 'Fifteen seconds. Hopefully we got away with it.'

'Now what happens?' Nina demanded. 'Who was that?'

'Field office for the FBI's Joint Terrorism Task Force,' said Kyle. 'They've been monitoring the airwaves for the past week waiting for my call. And I just ruined their night.'

'What was all that about a tornado?'

Kyle's shoulders sagged a little. 'Our team's code for an airborne biological weapon.'

TWENTY-FIVE

A chill wormed its way up Nina's spine. 'What biological weapon?'

'I didn't tell you everything, back at the barn,' said Kyle.

Nina glared at him, her hands on her hips. 'Explain.'

She watched Kyle pace the room, his impatience evident. He appeared to debate within himself whether to tell her; then he sighed.

'We've reason to believe the owner of the property next to Ross's is planning a terrorist attack on San Francisco,' he said quietly.

Nina snorted. 'With drugs?'

He shook his head. 'The drugs are only a small part of it,' he said. 'He's got men refining drugs for other people, making a *lot* of money from it. That funds his other project – the real reason they're out here.'

'What's he really doing?' asked Nina, her breathing ragged.

'By leaving the crops unharvested near the road and along the boundary with Ross's property, he's managed to disguise the fact that every single castor oil plant near the house and outbuildings has been stripped and not replaced,' he said. 'He's been refining it, into ricin.'

Nina wracked her memory. Her lip quivered. 'He's made a poison?'

Kyle nodded. 'We've never seen so much in one place,' he said.

'What will he do with it?'

'His men have filled the truck with the finished product. They're planning to deliver it to a distribution warehouse on the edge of the city. From there, Hudson's contacts will access the underground stations on the Bay Area Rapid Transit system. It means the ricin will be an airborne agent – there'll be mass casualties. They have new chemical and biological agent identification systems in place, but ricin's hard to detect.'

Nina covered her mouth with her hand. 'I don't get it. Why would they do that?'

Kyle sighed and ran a hand through his wet hair. 'When we did the background checks on Hudson, we found out that he'd been exposed to depleted uranium when he'd served in the first Gulf War. By the time the government stopped arguing with the medical community whether they were culpable or not, it was too late. Hudson had developed inoperable lung cancer.'

'That doesn't explain why Hudson would attack his own country though.'

'To any rational person it wouldn't, but Hudson's not. He's dying.' He shrugged. 'We believe it's because he blames America for his death. For not ensuring he was provided for when he came home. All Hudson knew was how to be a Marine, and the government wasn't interested in supporting him after his job was done.'

'Will he succeed?'

'If we don't stop him, yes. Inhalation of ricin isn't always fatal, but can you imagine the panic he'll cause?'

'When did you find out what was really going on?'

'Three months ago, when I went in undercover. Because of my alias, Hudson trusted me very quickly and brought me into his inner circle.'

'Why the hell didn't you tell me this before?'

His gaze met hers. 'I didn't know if I could trust you.'

———

The engine coughed once, sending a trail of blue smoke into the air, and a rattle shook the vehicle.

Kyle cursed and twisted the key again.

The starter motor whirred before the engine caught, properly this time, and the radio blared to life.

Nina lurched forward in her seat, shocked at the

sudden noise, hit the "off" button, and willed her heartbeat
to slow down. Her hands shook as she reached across and
fastened her seatbelt as the vehicle gathered speed.

'I always did hate country and western,' she grumbled.

After Kyle had alerted his superiors on the UHF radio,
Nina had left the mud room and wandered back through
the house, shocked at the damage that had been caused by
the intruders.

Entering the large living area with its stone fireplace
filling the opposite wall, Nina's heart sank as her gaze
swept over the ripped upholstery and overturned furniture.

She'd crouched and picked up a broken photo frame,
carefully extracted the photograph, and smoothed its
creases between her fingers.

In it, a much younger Ross stood with his father,
brother, and mother. Nina's mind worked the math, and
she realized the photo had been taken only a few months
before Ross's mother had passed away.

Standing, she crossed the room and propped up the
photograph on the mantelpiece.

'I'll put this right, Suzanne, don't worry,' she
whispered. 'Somehow, I'll put this right.'

She'd spun round at the sound of footsteps, and Kyle
entered the room.

Energy had radiated from him as he strode across the
carpet to her.

'They'll be tracking the vehicle now,' he said. 'Full
biohazard and SWAT teams should be on their way.'

'Will they stop it?'

'I hope so. They'd mobilize every available unit and coordinate with the emergency services. The ports will be closed down, and there'll be extra security at the airport in case anyone tries to make a run for it.'

He'd followed her gaze to the photograph.

'We can't go to Hudson's and check on them as well as make sure Ross is okay, Nina. There isn't time.'

She closed her eyes. 'If something happened to Tim and Jeff and I could've prevented it, Ross would never forgive me.' She bit her lip. 'I couldn't forgive myself.' She opened her eyes and turned to the FBI agent. 'I have to find out if they're okay, Kyle.'

'Come on then. Let's go.'

Now, he cursed when the vehicle reached the end of the driveway to the Flanagan property and the brakes squealed in protest.

'Christ, they're going to hear us a mile away.'

'What do you want to do?'

He fell silent for a moment, then slipped the engine into gear and moved forward.

'Get as close as we can and then walk.'

Kyle drove one-handed, letting his arm rest in his lap to take the pressure off his injured shoulder.

Nina held on to the armrest while he manoeuvred the vehicle around the flooded ruts in the track, the pick-up truck rocking from side to side as the worn tires tried to grip the slippery surface.

Behind them, an array of tools and assorted junk slid across the bench seat, clattering to the floor when the vehicle crashed down one steep rut and into another.

'I got the impression Ross liked order,' growled Kyle as he glared at the mess in the rear-view mirror.

Nina squinted through the rain lashing against the pitted windshield, her fingernails digging into the worn fabric of her seat. She held her breath as the truck slammed into another pothole.

'This is Tim's,' she said through gritted teeth. 'He's not so organized.'

TWENTY-SIX

Nina tapped her fingers on the dashboard, beating an unsteady rhythm while Kyle used the binoculars he'd taken from the Flanagan property and peered out the open window of the vehicle.

Below, Hudson's property was a hive of activity.

A low one-storey building was built to the left-hand side of the house, its roof a patchwork mess of corrugated iron in various stages of decay.

The huge double doors had been thrown open, light from within spilling onto the vehicles parked at its entrance.

A small group of men moved between the vehicles and the building, carrying boxes.

The house was a typical ranch design, with low eaves sheltering stone walls and a wooden deck that stretched around the building. Lights shone from the windows, casting elongated strips of light onto the surrounding mud-strewn lawn.

Three more buildings had been erected behind the house – another barn, and then a structure that resembled the Flanagan's machine shed, with the exception that Hudson's tractors seemed to have been out of use for some time, tarpaulins draped over their metal carcasses.

The last building appeared to be a storage shed, its doors closed to the elements.

Kyle had opened his door and balanced on the running board, raising himself above the roof to better see, before sliding back into his seat.

Nina stopped tapping and faced him. 'Well?'

He sighed. 'There are armed guards around the perimeter,' he said. 'Two more on the entrance to the house.'

'Who are all those men?' whispered Nina. 'I thought it would only be Hudson and a couple of other people.'

Kyle stared out the windshield, his face betraying no emotion. 'Ex-military,' he said. 'Hudson's attracted a lot of men who came home from overseas deployment and then found no-one wanted them. There aren't enough jobs to go around. Some of those men joined up as teenagers – they don't know any other way of life.'

He sighed and looked at his hands. 'Hudson runs the place like a cult. He preys on the weak and vulnerable. Some of those guys – what they've seen and what they've had to deal with at a young age – they're a mess.'

Nina noted the tinge of sadness in his voice. 'You wanted to help them, didn't you?'

He nodded. 'Unfortunately, Hudson's made sure they're beyond help,' he said. 'He lets them take drugs – the ones they're refining and selling to fund Hudson's plan.'

'But if they're stoned out of their minds, they'll be easier to get past, won't they?'

'No,' said Kyle. 'Hudson's much cleverer than that. He doesn't let them near the marijuana – most of the men down there are on speed or ice.' He turned to Nina. 'You need to understand – they're highly alert, burned out from lack of sleep, and paranoid.'

Nina looked at the property below, realising why the special agent was so concerned.

'What's going on down there?'

'It looks like they're getting ready to leave. Permanently.'

'I can't see the truck you mentioned.'

'That means it definitely made it across the highway before the landslide hit.' Kyle slapped his palm against the steering wheel. 'Thank God we managed to call it in.'

'Any sign of Jeff and Tim?'

'No. Not that I can see from here.'

'Then we have to get closer, right?'

Kyle rubbed his hands over his face, and for the first time in hours, Nina saw the weariness wash over him.

She reached out, placing her hand on his arm. 'Are you okay?'

He grunted from behind his fingers, then dropped his hands to his lap and stretched his neck. 'Yeah. Just thinking.'

'What?'

'That I've had case officers less demanding than you.'

Nina withdrew her hand and frowned. 'Sorry. I-I thought that was your plan. To come here and rescue Ross's family with the rest of your men.'

Kyle snorted.

'What did I say?' Nina fought down the panic that had sent her heartbeat into free-fall. 'What's wrong?'

He sighed. 'I didn't want to tell you,' he said, looking at his hands. 'When I spoke to headquarters... Look, their main focus has to be stopping that truck. If the ricin reaches those underground air ducts – you can imagine what will happen.'

'But they're sending someone to help you here, right? We're going to find out what's happened to Ross's family?'

'They're not coming, Nina.' He turned to face her, his jaw set. 'Not until the truck's secure.'

'But that could take hours!'

'I know. I'm fully aware of that. They don't have the manpower to spare. It was always the plan. They won't come here until they find that truck and it's been secured.'

'Isn't there anything you can do?'

Kyle beat his fist against the glass window. He finally spoke.

'Look, I'll go down there. Check the licence plates. At least then, my office can put out a trace on them. Even if they're interstate by the time they do, they can use local law enforcement to track them in the meantime.'

'Why can't you get the local police to help us now?'

'Because we don't know if any of those vehicles down there contain ricin as well, Nina,' he said. 'Because the local authorities can't possibly deal with a biological weapon, you understand?'

Nina swallowed and then looked out the windshield to the property below. 'Kyle, if they're packing up to move out, then they're going to make sure they cover their tracks, aren't they?'

She heard him exhale, but he didn't answer.

'So, your lot will stop the truck, and they can *try* to track the vehicles down there, but chances are, they won't catch the people who did this. And,' she said, her hands trembling as she unclipped her seatbelt, 'if those people down there are good at covering their tracks, they're going to kill Ross's father and brother to make sure they don't talk, aren't they?'

She reached for the door.

'Where are you going?'

Nina stopped, her hand on the door handle, and glared at him. 'If you're not going to do something, I am. I can't sit here while you let them murder two innocent people.'

She pulled on the handle, then gasped as Kyle's arm shot out, reaching across her body and pinning her to the seat.

'Fuck!' His hand dropped away, and he fell back into his seat, clutching his shoulder and swearing profusely.

Nina cursed and slammed the door shut. 'Are you okay?'

Kyle grimaced and shifted in his seat.

'Do you want me to take another look at your shoulder?'

'No.'

'I'm sorry,' she said, fighting back tears. 'But I can't sit here and let them kill Ross's family.'

His jaw clenched, the muscles in his neck growing taut.

Nina leaned forward and beat the dashboard with her fists. 'Dammit, Kyle. Talk to me! You burst into my home in the middle of a storm, you drag me into your whole secret operation that goes wrong, I get shot at – God knows what's happened to Ross – and then you just clam up?' She twisted in her seat to face him. 'Talk to me!'

She threw herself back into her seat, then wiped at her cheeks, hot tears stinging her eyes.

'Hey, I'm sorry.'

He leaned towards her, but she drew back out of his reach.

'Don't,' she said. 'Either you tell me how you're going to make this right, or I'm going down there on my own.'

She pursed her lips, angry with herself for blowing up at him, and furious with him for being so under control in such desperate conditions. She knew it was his training, but the way he could stay so outwardly calm while she fell apart was unnerving.

Kyle remained silent, his eyes tracking the movement of the men below.

Nina's gaze followed his. 'How the hell are we going to do this?' she whispered.

'I don't know,' he said. 'My cover's blown, so it's not as if I can just walk in there and expect a happy reunion.'

'And you've only got me to help. Not a great scenario, is it?' Nina held her breath. She could feel the tension emanating off the man next to her.

'Alright,' he said eventually. 'We'll go down there to see if we *can* do something. We'll stay in the shadows, move slowly.' He reached across and put his hand on Nina's arm. 'I can't say this enough. You need to do everything I tell you, no hesitating. You understand?'

Her gaze met his, and she was shocked at the change in his demeanour despite his light touch. The adrenaline of the chase had kicked in. His eyes blazed, and his shoulders were set, as if he'd never been stabbed. Was this what he was like undercover? Was this how he coped with what he did?

She nodded mutely.

'Okay,' he said. 'Let's go.'

TWENTY-SEVEN

Nina peered over her shoulder as the last of the lightning storm streaked across the far end of the valley hundreds of miles away.

Clouds scuttled across the sky, the worst of the rainfall following in their wake, while a final rumble in the distance reached her ears.

She shivered. Her feet were soaked, the thin leather of her ankle boots no match for the terrain they'd been subjected to the past few hours. Her clothes stuck to her, and the cold drizzle froze her skin, creating an ache in her bones she knew she'd feel for days – if she survived the night.

She'd last looked at her watch in the car, the dial at two o'clock, confirming her weariness and exhaustion.

Kyle walked ahead of her, his fingers laced through

hers, guiding her through the undergrowth as they approached Hudson's property.

She had learned more about Ross's neighbour as they left the vehicle hidden by the side of the road, covering it with branches to disguise its outline.

The FBI agent had been sickened by Hudson's attitude, the way he'd preyed on disillusioned and vulnerable ex-soldiers, young men who were lost in their own country, with no skills except to follow orders.

'A lot of them look up to him, like he's some sort of father figure,' Kyle explained. 'Except that when it's time for him to escape, he'll probably ditch the whole lot of them to face their fate alone.'

Nina had sensed his frustration and anger then, and as she stumbled after him in the darkness down the ridge and closer to the property, she wondered what drove him, what kept him going when all seemed lost.

Kyle had fallen silent, and Nina glanced across at him.

'Are you okay? Is your shoulder hurting?'

He shook his head.

She bit her lip, seeing his jaw clench as he ran his hand over the stubble on his chin, watching the activity around Hudson's house. For a moment, she couldn't work out his reticence – he'd been so in control and focused before. Now, deep lines creased his forehead as he glared at the movement of men and vehicles, their shouts traveling in waves over the gusts of wind that rustled the tree branches above them.

Then she realized. The thought terrified her until she remembered Ross, back at the truck stop, sacrificing himself so she and Kyle could escape.

'You can't do this on your own, can you?'

He sighed. 'No. No, I can't.'

'I can help.'

'You probably can. Except I'm not used to being responsible for someone, Nina. Not like this.'

She heard the tremor in his voice, the uncertainty emanating from him. She took a deep breath to stop her voice from shaking.

'You don't have a choice.'

He turned his gaze back to Hudson's property, his eyes flickering over the men moving only a few hundred metres in front of them, beyond the treeline. 'I do. I can leave you here.'

'That's ridiculous. You don't stand a chance on your own.'

'If I take you, I'm going to be watching *your* back, as well as mine.'

Nina took a deep breath. 'Kyle, I can't stand here doing nothing. Ross...' She cleared her throat. 'Ross didn't stay behind so I could run and hide,' she said, her voice stronger. 'What do you need me to do?'

'Okay,' he said. 'I need you to learn fifteen years' worth of training in about five minutes. And that isn't going to happen. So we're going to have to do the best we can with what we've got.'

He reached down to his ankle and pulled.

Nina's eyes opened wide at the vicious-looking knife he held out to her.

'Something else John left for me,' he said, waving it at her. 'Take it.'

'What do you want me to do?'

He pointed across the wide expanse of the paddock. 'I need you to slash the tires on as many vehicles as you can. Stay low. Two tires per vehicle at least.'

Nina felt her throat constrict. She looked at the parked cars and pick-up trucks. Eight vehicles in total, with the last two nearest the sprawling house.

From their position, she could see that the veranda was in darkness, patches of light shining through gaps in blinds and curtains. The guards' silhouettes flickered between the windows as they patrolled the outer perimeter of the house, rifles poised.

She turned back to Kyle.

He was still crouched, holding out the knife to her. 'Can you do this for me?'

'Yes.' She reached out with a shaking hand.

'Good girl.'

'Where will you be?'

'I'm going to recce the perimeter of the house. See if Hudson's there. Find out how many men he's got guarding him.'

'Ross's family?'

'Yes, them too. But I can't do anything for them until I know what the situation is.'

'Won't the guards see you?'

'I'm going to follow them, leave a bit of space so they don't hear me over this rain.'

Nina nodded. The rain on the painted tin roof of the ranch would easily mask any noise Kyle made. He'd just have to make sure he stayed out of sight.

'I'm going to go now, okay?'

She nodded.

'Good. Count to sixty; then you make a start. I'll meet you back here.'

She opened her mouth to ask him how long he'd be, but he'd already disappeared into the shadows.

Within moments, she'd lost sight of him, and then remembered she should have been counting.

As she counted off the sixtieth second, she took a deep breath, then poked her head round the side of the vehicle she'd been sheltering behind and squinted through the darkness.

She held her breath, waiting for the now familiar flash of activity in front of the windows as the guards made their next pass, then stood and ran towards the nearest vehicle, keeping her body low.

Moving fast, expecting to hear a shout or a gunshot at any moment, she reached the abandoned car and crouched next to the front wheel, keeping the vehicle between her and the house, blocking the guards' view of her.

Without waiting to see if she'd been noticed, she pulled out the knife and rammed it into the rubber surface next to her.

The tire wall burst with a sharp *pop* as the point of the knife made contact and then hissed as the air began to escape.

Nina froze, straining to hear over the wind and rain, sure that the sound had carried towards the guards. She raised her head above the trunk of the car, searching for any movement. The guards moved away along the side of the house, oblivious to her actions.

When she realized she hadn't been discovered, she pushed the knife in up to its hilt, leaning against it with her weight to make sure it pierced all the way through, then tugged it out and scuttled along the length of the car to the next tire.

Once both tires had been slashed, she cautiously peered around the hood of the car.

The guards had disappeared from view.

Nina bit her lip, peered across at the next car only a few paces from where she crouched, and considered taking a chance.

Her heart leapt painfully at a cough from the direction of the house, and she ducked.

Over the noise of the rain, she heard one of the guards laugh, and the scent of a freshly lit cigarette wafted across to her.

She counted to thirty, and then raised her head above the hood.

The veranda was deserted.

She ran, sliding to a stop behind the second car, quickly applied the knife to the tires, and kept going.

Ten minutes later, she'd attacked all but two of the vehicles.

The second to last one, a pick-up truck, had been parked facing the house, both sides exposed.

Nina cursed under her breath. No matter how she approached it she would be seen by the guards or anyone else at the house, as well as anyone approaching the house from the outlying buildings.

She turned her attention to the vehicle beyond it, which lay in darkness, parked the furthest from the house. It looked like an old four-door wagon. She checked over her shoulder, back towards the damaged vehicles she'd left in her wake, and made her decision.

Launching herself across the paddock, she pumped her arms and ran as fast as she could at the vehicle, all the while expecting gunshots to ring out from the veranda.

On the verge of exhaustion, she slid to the ground next to the vehicle, her feet losing traction in the mud. She clenched her fingers around the knife, desperate not to drop it – not now. Not yet.

Her breathing laboured, she gave herself a few seconds to recover, then faced the back wheel. The darkness enveloped her so far from the house lights, and she moved her fingers across the rubber surface, tracing the outline until she found the inner part of the tire wall, next to the rusting hub cap.

Changing her grip on the knife, she wedged it into the material, wiggling it when the familiar *pop* had passed, trying to get the weapon deeper into the tire.

Then the knife gave way under her, and she felt rather than heard the *snap* that shuddered up the shaft.

For a moment, she sat, shocked, unwilling to comprehend what had happened. She leaned her forehead against the bodywork of the vehicle and closed her eyes.

A shaking breath escaped from her lips, and when she raised her head and squinted through the darkness, she wiggled the knife from side to side.

The hilt fell from the tire, a stubby remnant of the blade sticking out from the end.

'Shit.'

Nina held the knife up, trying to gauge how much was left. She gingerly moved her fingers up the flat side of the blade and realized only a tiny amount remained.

She clenched her teeth and changed her position until she could see the last remaining vehicle.

Kyle's instructions echoed in her mind.

Two tires per vehicle at least.

Would it make a difference if she only slashed one tire on this vehicle and managed to damage the last one? Would Hudson's men be able to still use the car with one damaged tire?

Could she even make it across the paddock to reach the
four-wheel drive that sat, taunting her?

As she churned her options around in her head,
wondering whether she should attempt to get to the vehicle
and use the broken blade to try and slice through the tires,
a thick arm snaked around her shoulders and a large hand
clamped across her mouth.

Her eyes opened wide, and she began to struggle,
trying to loosen the man's grip.

He swore, a low growl that she felt between her
shoulder blades.

'For fuck's sake, it's me,' Kyle hissed.

TWENTY-EIGHT

Hudson swept the paperwork from his desk, reached behind the abandoned chair, and pulled a plastic tube towards himself.

'What's that?' asked the younger man leaning against the wall. He moved forward as he watched the older man uncap the tube and extract a rolled-up document.

'Construction plans, Brad,' said Hudson. 'For this place.'

He flattened the plans with the palm of his hand, then grabbed two desk ornaments and used them to pin down opposite corners.

The younger man approached the desk, frowning. 'Why?'

Hudson glanced up at him, a gleam in his eye. 'Because when we leave here, I want no trace left behind. Nothing.' He loosened his cuff buttons and rolled his shirt sleeves up to his elbows, then shoved his hands in his pockets and stared at the plans. 'If the Feds are on to us, then they're going to get a surprise when they show up here.'

He caught movement out the corner of his eye as Larry entered the room, nodded at Brad, then started towards the desk.

A smile flickered across Hudson's face. 'Ah, the explosives expert is here.'

'Jock.'

'Where've you been, Larry?'

'Checking the perimeter of the house.'

'Anything to report?'

'Nothing.'

'Good.' Hudson inclined his head towards the plans on the desk. 'Does this help?'

Brad stood aside as Larry moved round the desk and leaned forward, tracing his fingers over the outlines of the building.

'Do you have plans for the basement as well?'

Hudson reached into the plastic tube and pulled out another rolled-up document. 'Yes. And drawings of the roof structure.'

'I'll need them all.'

'What are you going to do?' Brad's eyes moved from one man to the other. 'You're not thinking of blowing this place up, are you?'

'That's exactly what we're going to do,' said Hudson.

'No traces, remember?' He turned to Larry. 'How much time do you need?'

The explosives expert shrugged. 'An hour, maybe two.'

Hudson checked his watch. 'Our ride will be here at zero-five-hundred hours,' he said. 'Be done and clear by zero-four-hundred at the latest.'

'I'll make a start.'

He leaned forward, rolled up the plans, and tucked them under his arm.

Hudson watched the man leave the room and then turned to Brad.

'Follow him,' he said. 'Make sure he sets all the charges.'

Brad frowned. 'Don't you trust him?'

'I trusted Kyle Roberts,' growled Hudson. 'Look where that got me.' He leaned down, picked up a briefcase, and began shoveling documents into it. 'Go. See what he's up to. And make sure you tell everyone we're leaving at five,' he said, and nodded towards the door. 'They don't want to get left behind if they want to live.'

Brad nodded, his eyes wide, and jogged from the room.

Hudson checked his watch and resumed packing.

In a way, he hoped the Feds did show up. Then he could really teach them to mind their own business.

TWENTY-NINE

'What the hell were you trying to do?'

Nina glared at the shadow of a man in front of her.

Their laboured breathing slowed as one.

'I didn't want to surprise you and have you yell out.'

'So, you thought you'd give me a heart attack instead, is that it?'

'Hey, I didn't know you were going to fight me,' he snapped.

Nina sat back on her heels, ignoring the damp that was seeping through the knees of her jeans. She glared at him as he shuffled closer until he was sheltered alongside her, their backs against the bodywork of the car. 'You scared the shit out of me.'

A sigh escaped from the man next to her, and she decided to change the subject. 'Did you do the recce? What's going on over there?'

'They're packing up to leave.'

'You mean they're going to escape?'

'Not if I can help it.' He craned his neck until he could see past her and squinted at the line of vehicles. 'How did you get on?'

'Fine, until the knife broke on this tire.' She jabbed her chin towards the four-wheel drive. 'I didn't get to that one.'

'That's not so bad. Nice work.'

'Thanks. Now what do we do?'

He leaned his head back against the car and stretched. 'I need to get inside. It looks like there are two men moving around inside the house; I'm not sure what they're doing, but the rest of Hudson's men look as if they've got bags packed. Like they're ready to roll out.'

'What about Hudson?'

'In the study. Running paperwork through a shredder.'

'Evidence?'

He shrugged. 'Probably. But I've got enough to prove what he's been doing, so I'm not too worried about that.'

'Jeff and Tim?'

'I couldn't see them, so I'm assuming they're being kept out of the way.'

Nina pushed her fingers through her hair. 'That makes things difficult, doesn't it?'

'Yes,' he said. 'I've got two guns. I need to kill six men. Plus, Hudson. Without getting killed myself, so I can rescue Jeff and Tim.'

Nina swallowed. He'd said it so clinically, so devoid of emotion.

'There's something else,' he said.

'What?'

'Sean and Dani are here. Come on.'

Nina shivered, her blood running cold, and a keen hatred began to worm its way into her veins as she realized that, no matter what happened tonight, she wanted only one thing.

To make sure Ross's family got out alive, even if she hadn't been able to save him.

She ran after Kyle, her fingers interlaced with his so she didn't become separated from him.

They used the shadows beyond the vehicles to move around the outer perimeter of the property, running in short bursts between the guards' patrol.

Before they'd left the shelter of the four-door station wagon, the front door to the property had opened, light flooding over the pathway beyond.

Two men had stepped out and exchanged words with the guards, who had then disappeared back into the confines of the house.

'Shift change,' Kyle had murmured.

They'd waited until the new guards had turned their backs before making their escape.

Now, they moved in the darkness, slipping and sliding over the uneven ground, gradually circling the ranch and its inhabitants.

In between bursts of running, she had time to take in her surroundings. The ranch was different from the building she remembered as a teenager.

The previous owners had been elderly, merely using the property as a small-holding, slowly leaving the outlying fields to fallow and retreating to a small vegetable garden more easily tended as the drought intensified. Only the fields closest to the house had been bankable crops, and mostly cattle fodder at that.

Hudson had apparently kept up appearances by maintaining the cattle crops, but the vegetable patch had been laid to waste, and as Nina followed Kyle around its perimeter, the earthy stench of abandoned soil reached her senses, seconds before she tripped and fell.

She pushed herself into a crouching position and glared at the protruding tree root that had felled her.

Rubbing her ankle, she frowned, realising her error, then raised her head and gazed up.

No tree large enough to match the root towered above; there were only scrubby saplings that had failed to grow during the drought-stricken years of late. She reached forward, her interest piqued, and touched the tree root. Despite its muddy appearance, it seemed soft under her fingers, and pliant.

'No!' Kyle dropped beside her, pushed her hand out of the way, and hissed into her ear, 'Don't touch it!'

Nina frowned, confused.

He peered over her shoulder, towards the house, then

229

reached down and cupped his hand around the bulb of the flashlight before switching it on and aiming it at the tree root.

Nina recoiled in horror.

The matted body of a large dog lay partially covered in leaf mulch, its eyes and muzzle festering with busy maggots. Mud covered its once-glossy golden coat.

'Oh, God.' Nina covered her mouth with her hand, the stench of the dog's wasted body searing her nose.

'Sorry.' Kyle flicked off the torch. 'But I couldn't let you touch it.'

'It's not an *it*, it's a *her*. It's Misty, Ross's dog,' said Nina. She moved away. 'What happened to her?'

'I wasn't involved,' said Kyle. 'Hudson wasn't happy about it, but he did it without me anyway. He's got enough sick bastards willing to do his dirty work.'

Nina folded her arms across her chest. 'What did he do to her?'

Kyle sighed. 'He wanted to make sure the poison worked. So, they tried some of it on the dog.'

'Jesus.' Nina spun round and walked several paces away.

'Wait.' Kyle followed and grabbed her sleeve. 'I couldn't stop him. I had to let it play out.'

'Play out?' Nina sputtered. 'This isn't a *game*. What sort of sick bastard poisons a dog on purpose?'

Kyle let go of her arm. 'The same sort of sick bastard

who's going to do this to a whole city,' he said, his voice shaking with anger. 'So, can we get a move on?'

He stood back and held out his hand.

She shook her head, exasperated, took his hand, and stalked behind him, following him around the perimeter until he stopped and pulled her closer.

He reached into his waistband and pulled out one of the guns. He checked the magazine, slotted it back into place, and flicked the safety to "on", then held it out to her.

She raised her hand to take it from him, but he jerked it out of her reach at the last minute.

'Don't shoot anyone unless you're threatened, okay? It's for emergencies only.'

'I'll try to remember that. Hand it over.'

'Can you actually use one of these?'

'It's been a while, but I think I can remember.'

Kyle grinned and handed over the weapon.

'What? What's so funny?'

'I heard you say something similar about riding a motorbike,' he said, the skin at his eyes creasing.

Nina gave a short laugh. 'Yes, I did, didn't I?'

'You're full of surprises, Nina,' he said. 'I like that.'

231

THIRTY

Jock Hudson turned the glass in his hand, condensation running down the crystal and pooling onto the oak-colored table.

He raised the drink and closed his eyes as the amber liquid burned his throat and soothed his nerves. Ice cubes cooled his lips, contrasting with the bourbon. The chair creaked under his weight as he opened his eyes and leaned forward, his fingers reaching for the uncapped bottle.

He'd been so damn close. He cursed in frustration as he poured another measure into the glass, then screwed the lid into place and shoved the bottle across the table out of reach.

He rubbed a hand across his face.

He'd never known a storm like this, despite traveling the world with the military. Lightning, thunder, sure, but not a drought-breaker like this one. Not in a contained valley where the static from the lightning scrambled satellite signals and high winds tore down phone lines.

The lack of progress by his hunters frustrated him. His only consolation was that they'd caught up with John as he'd been driving the car towards town.

As for the other escapee, no-one knew, and that made him nervous.

His man had returned, reporting he'd shot the lying bastard but that Kyle had tumbled from the ridge, and there was no way of checking in the dark, not over that terrain.

Hudson cursed and took another gulp of his drink.

He'd lost his touch. He'd been so wrapped up in the final stages of the project he hadn't made sure his men had conducted the proper background checks on the two men when they'd shown up three months ago. Instead, he'd been grateful for the extra help, his ego inflated by the lies they'd spun him about their own military backgrounds and their eagerness to join his cause.

As he placed the glass on the table, his hands trembled. He glared at them, as if that would stop the shaking from reaching his arms.

Not this. Not now.

Hudson tipped his head back, swallowed the last of the bourbon, and shoved his chair back, then stood and squared his shoulders.

He walked to the sink, rinsed the glass, and left it upside down on the counter, then shook his head at the habit.

Within four hours, there'd be no house, let alone a kitchen counter to worry about.

His head jerked sideways at a noise from the passageway, and his hand fell to the pistol tucked into his belt, his thumb flicking the safety catch off.

Brad appeared, his face sweaty.

Hudson relaxed. 'What is it?'

'Just getting some water for Larry,' he explained, wiping his forehead. 'He's nearly finished laying the charges in the roof. You wouldn't believe how stuffy it is up there.'

'These old ranch houses were built to last,' said Hudson. 'And keep the warmth in. Tell Larry to make sure he has the charges right under the supporting beams; otherwise it'll never work.'

The younger man nodded, filled two glasses from the tap, and turned back to the door.

'Brad?'

'Yeah?'

'What do you think? Do you trust him?'

'What do you mean?'

Hudson shrugged. 'He showed up two months before the others.'

He didn't need to say who. They'd all been shocked at

the revelation the small group had been infiltrated by the FBI.

'Yeah, I trust him,' said Brad. He shrugged. 'He wouldn't be doing such a good job of covering your tracks otherwise.'

Hudson grunted and waved the man away.

Hudson's eyes narrowed as one of his other men approached, an older man in tow, his shoulders slumped, worry lines creasing his brow.

'Did it work, Peter?'

His security man nodded. 'Perfect,' he said, jerking his head at the older man. 'He did as he was told, just like you said he would.'

'Good.' Hudson's mouth twisted as he narrowed his eyes at the farmer. 'For a moment there, I didn't think it would work. Did he suspect anything?'

'No,' said Peter. 'It's amazing how trusting people will be when they're desperate.'

The two men laughed.

'So you'll let my boy go now?' Jeff Flanagan surged forward, his face hopeful.

'Not a chance in hell.' The humour left Hudson's voice as he glared at the man.

'But you said you'd let him go if I helped you.' Jeff looked from one man to the other in bewilderment. 'You promised.'

'I lied.'

'You can't do that!'

Hudson sneered, his voice dangerously low. 'I can do whatever I want,' he snarled. He jerked his chin towards the door. 'Take him away. Put him with his boy. He's no use to me now.'

THIRTY-ONE

Nina mimicked Kyle's crouched stance as they broke through the treeline and tore across the unguarded perimeter towards the smaller of the ramshackle buildings.

Compared to the newer barn closer to the house, the sheds appeared derelict and unused since the property's previous owners had moved on, taking their more traditional farming methods with them.

Kyle seized her arm, wrenched open the door to a wooden shed, and pushed her inside.

'What are you doing?' asked Nina once Kyle had let go of her arm.

'We need a distraction so I can get into the house,' said Kyle, and pulled the door shut.

With no windows to give away their position, he switched on the flashlight and left it on the workbench, its bulb flickering as the battery life began to drain from it. He hurried over to the far side of the large shed and started to run his hands over the steel drums stored along one side of the building. He patted his pocket and cursed.

'What are you looking for?' asked Nina as she approached.

'Anything that's highly flammable,' he said, and then pointed to the other side of the shed. 'Take a look over there – we need something with alcohol in it, or any other flammable liquid. And if you see a box of matches or a cigarette lighter, put it somewhere safe. The one I took from John must've fallen out when we were on the bike.'

Nina put the gun on the workbench and began to search the shelves alongside, pulling down plastic tubs of liquid and reading the warning labels on the sides before discarding the ones they couldn't use.

'Okay, what have you got?'

She glanced up as Kyle appeared next to her. 'Not much.' She gestured to the small collection of bottles set to one side.

He began to pick up the bottles and then looked over his shoulder at the drums he'd rolled to one side, away from the others.

'What are you thinking?'

'I need something to act as a fuse,' he said. 'Those drums have diesel in them. Enough to create the distraction I need, but without a fuse, they're useless.'

'Where are you going to put them?'

'Inside the door. We need a fuse so we can get far

enough away from the explosion.' He rubbed his hand over his chin. 'And the ground's wet outside, so we can't pour anything onto the floor and expect to light it.'

'What about this?' Nina held up a large bottle of liquid soap.

'No good – like I said, you can't put it on the ground.' He turned away.

'It might work if you rub it along the walls of the building, look.' She squirted some of the liquid onto her fingers and held up her hand to Kyle. The soap stuck, without dripping onto the floor. 'The roof has eaves. It'll protect the soap from being washed off by the rain.'

He frowned, staring at her fingers, before his lips twitched. 'What's the alcohol content in that stuff?'

He reached over and grabbed the bottle, squinting in the poor light.

'It's a lot,' said Nina. 'It's the industrial stuff they use to get grease off their fingers when they've been working on the machinery.'

She grabbed a cloth and wiped her hands.

'Is there any more of this?'

Nina stepped back and raised her chin until she could see the top shelf. 'Yes – up there.'

'Okay. We need to mix it with something, though, to give it a boost.'

Kyle reached up, grabbed the second bottle of soap, and then began to search through the other bottles Nina had collected. 'Nothing here.'

He jogged over to the opposite side of the shed, away from the drums, where a collection of hessian bags had been stacked against the wall. He ran his hands over the printed text on the outside of a half-full bag, then picked it up and returned to the workbench, a grin on his face.

'Fertilizer?' Nina's eyes widened.

'Well, we wanted a distraction, right?' He hefted the bag onto the workbench. 'Ammonia nitrate will work a treat. Find something we can use as a mixing bowl,' he said. 'You're going to have to help me.'

'Isn't this dangerous?'

His eyes shone through the gloom. 'Yes.'

'You're enjoying this, aren't you?'

He shrugged. 'I need to stop them.'

'We could die.'

'Yes, we could.' He placed his hands on her shoulders. 'But I can't do this without you,' he said. 'So, will you help me?'

'Yes,' she said, her voice shaking. She cleared her throat. 'Yes,' she said more clearly. 'Of course, I will.'

Kyle grinned. 'Good.' He gave her shoulders a final squeeze and then held up the bowl. 'Let's cook,' he said, before pointing to the workbench. 'Add the soap first.'

Nina tipped the liquid into the container. 'How much?'

'All of it – both bottles.'

She squeezed the contents of the second bottle into the container while Kyle unwrapped the top of the hessian bag. She paused to watch as he put his hand inside and then withdrew it. A pale pink powder covered his palm.

'Is it dry?'

'Yes.' He pushed her gently to one side, before adding two handfuls of the powder to the soap. 'Okay, now I'll mix this together.'

'Is it safe?'

'At the moment. I don't want too much air getting into the mix, that's all.'

She watched, her heartbeat drumming in her ears as she watched him stir the fertilizer into the bowl with the soap.

He used a stick to mix the two elements together, then slowly poured in the diesel and stirred until the mixture thickened.

Nina moved away, seeking a distraction from the thought that they were about to be blown into oblivion if Kyle got the measurements wrong, and began to search the shelves for anything else they might need.

She busied herself pushing through the detritus strewn across the dusty shelving units, discarding small boxes of nails and assorted bolts. She recalled how Ross's father always kept his workshop tidy, berating the kids when they didn't put tools back in the right place or left things lying around. A smile flickered across her lips at the memory.

Finally, she heard Kyle drop the stick onto the workbench.

'We're ready.'

Nina held up the small box in her hand. 'Found something else for you too.'

'Matches?' He grinned. 'That's great – for a while there I thought we were going to have to do it the old-fashioned way with two sticks.'

'How do you know this?'

'What?'

'Making home-made bombs.'

'I usually try to stop them,' he said. 'I guess I've just remembered some of the stuff I've seen.'

'What will this do?'

Kyle leaned against the bench, cradling his shoulder. 'The fertilizer makes the soap thicker, so it'll stick to the wall better, as well as accelerating the diesel in the liquid. We'll leave a trail of it from those fuel drums, then out the shed and along the side of the walls. Once we know we can get away without being seen, we light the fuse and run for cover.'

'And then?'

'Then I get into the house while they're running to see what all the noise is about.'

Nina swallowed. 'What if it doesn't work? What if someone sees you?'

'I'll worry about that if it happens.' He moved closer and peered into the makeshift bowl. 'That'll do. We need to do this now. It's very unstable like this.'

He picked up the container before leading the way

towards the exit. Nina hung back as he opened the shed door, checking their escape route.

'Okay, come on,' he whispered. 'Hang on to the back of my shirt, and don't let go.'

Nina's hand shook as she wove her fingers into the pale blue cotton that poked out from under Kyle's jacket.

He moved quickly, giving Nina a fraction of a moment to shut the door behind them before he edged slowly along the wall of the building, smearing the sticky liquid on the surface as they progressed.

Reaching the back of the shed, Kyle dropped the bowl to the floor and held a match to the sticky substance. It flared, then caught and began to burn its way around the building.

Kyle grabbed Nina's hand and pulled her towards the treeline.

'Move!'

She slid to a halt behind a thick tree trunk, her breathing laboured, adrenaline kicking in, and peered round Kyle's shoulder, waiting for the explosion.

And waited.

'What's wrong?' she hissed. 'Why didn't it work?'

'I don't know. Maybe I missed a bit in the dark. Maybe the soap didn't stick as well as we thought it would.'

'What do we do now?'

She stared up at him, trying not to panic, seeking his assurance that he had another plan, another way they could get into the house and rescue Ross's family.

His jaw was set, his eyes refusing to meet hers, his gaze centred on the building behind her.

'Kyle?' She nudged him. 'I said, what are we going to do now?'

His eyes opened wide, and he pushed her between the shoulder blades – hard.

'Get down!'

THIRTY-TWO

Nina cried out as the shockwave tore past them, fractured timber and debris blasting through the treeline.

Kyle pushed her to the ground and lay prone over her, sheltering her face against his chest, his uninjured arm protecting the back of her head.

She screwed up her eyes as the heat rushed by them, Kyle's weight pressing her into the water-logged undergrowth.

As the initial blast abated, Kyle raised his head and shifted his body into a crouch.

Nina rolled over and joined him, pulling pieces of vegetation from her wet hair.

Beyond the treeline, the shed had disintegrated, spewing its contents across the paddock towards the new outbuildings.

Flames licked at the night sky, despite the fine drizzle

that still fell across the valley. Men were running towards the ruin, shouting and pointing.

'I think they know we're here now,' said Nina, as flames licked at the remnants of the outbuilding.

'Move!' hissed Kyle, and grabbed her arm, shading his eyes with his other hand.

He pulled her away from the inferno that engulfed the remnants of the wooden outbuilding and into the shadows behind the house.

While the flames still burned and Hudson's men ran to see what the commotion was about, they could take advantage of both the distraction and the fact the men's night vision would be severely impaired.

They ducked behind an old tractor, moments before two men ran past, the first shouting over his shoulder.

Nina turned her head at movement in the house to see a man standing in the front doorway, his hands on his hips as he surveyed the chaotic scene.

'Look,' she said, tapping Kyle's forearm.

He twisted to see where she pointed.

'Hudson,' he spat. He held out his hand. 'Come on. We need to move now if this is going to work.'

Nina peered at the figure on the porch as he stalked down the staircase towards his panicked men shouting orders; then she concentrated on where she was running as Kyle led her in a sweeping arc through the trees.

When the back door of the property came into view, he stopped.

'Here, give me your gun.'

Nina frowned and handed over the weapon. 'Why?'

Kyle jerked his chin towards the house. 'I want to take a look inside. I don't plan to get caught, but if I do, I want all the firepower I can get my hands on.'

He slipped the extra weapon into the waistband of his jeans.

'Kyle? What do you want me to do?'

A manic grin crossed his face as he looked down at her. 'Be good. Stay out of trouble.'

Nina stared at him, open-mouthed, as he jogged towards the house, cracked open the door, and slipped inside.

'Typical,' she muttered, crossing her arms and leaning against the knotted trunk to wait.

———

Kyle pushed the door shut and then stood in the large kitchen, blinking until his vision adjusted to the bright lights that swamped him.

Opposite, a large table contained the detritus of a meal consumed in a hurry, and he relished the thought of the panic that Hudson and his men must have felt when they realized their careful months of planning were in danger of falling apart at the last minute.

Three months of living in a cooped-up environment with such twisted individuals had taken a harder toll on

Kyle than he was prepared to admit to himself or anyone else.

He thought of Ross and Nina and the simple lives they lived in comparison and swore he'd put it right, that somehow he'd succeed, even if it meant he wouldn't survive.

He removed his boots and hid them inside a cupboard under the sink, not wanting to leave a trail of wet and muddy footprints through the house to signal his return to Hudson or his men, and padded in his bare feet across the tiled floor towards the passageway.

He kept his gun raised, the familiar weight in his two-handed grip small comfort against the mammoth task he faced.

He checked the front door, saw no-one approaching, and sprinted across the passageway to the living area.

A bare room, it held a pungent aroma of stale cigarette smoke and male sweat.

He trod carefully. Two of Hudson's thugs were occasional heroin users, and the last thing he wanted was to survive the next few hours only to die from an infection caused by standing on someone else's needle.

Satisfied the downstairs area was deserted, Kyle crept up the staircase, his back to the wall, working on the theory Hudson had locked Ross's father and brother in one of the bedrooms on the next floor.

Unlike the Flanagan property, the staircase was bare, the carpet pulled up years ago before it had rotted away.

Kyle held his breath every time one of his feet took his weight, hoping he remembered which stair treads were loose and liable to creak.

Reaching the top step without incident, he swept his gun left and right along the passageway and then moved.

A quick check of the rooms yielded no results and, exasperated, Kyle began to hurry back along the passageway.

He jerked his head up at a sudden noise and cursed, a moment before a man launched himself through an open hatchway to the attic and landed across his shoulders, knocking him to the floor.

Kyle swore as he tumbled onto his injured shoulder, dropping his gun in the process.

He rolled, kicking his assailant as he tried to move out of his way in the narrow space, and reached for the second weapon at his waistband.

'Don't.'

He raised his eyes and cursed. 'Larry. Nice of you to drop in.'

'Kyle.' A smile crossed the man's face, and he waggled the gun. 'Get up. Hudson's going to be pleased to see you.'

Kyle chuckled and put his hands on his head before standing. 'I don't think he will be.'

Larry leaned forward and tugged the second gun from Kyle's belt. 'Let's go and find out, shall we?'

THIRTY-THREE

'Don't move, or we'll shoot.'

Nina froze and then slowly raised her hands in the air.

She closed her eyes, her heart sinking. She realized she'd been so intent on watching the house, waiting for Kyle to return, that she'd failed to watch her own back. She cursed her stupidity.

'How many of you are there?'

'T-two.'

'Turn around.'

Nina opened her eyes and shuffled until she was facing the sound of the voice. She lowered her head, squinting against the bright flashlight beam that shone in her face.

'What's your name?'

'Nina O'Brien.'

The light remained in her face as a second dark shape moved forward and grabbed her arm.

'Stand still.'

Nina's heart pounded, her pulse in her ears and throat as the man moved his hands over her body, checking for weapons. She fought down the urge to vomit as his fingers lingered too long and stepped back out of his reach.

He lurched forward and grabbed her roughly by her hair, tipping her face up to his.

'You were told to stay still.'

Nina gagged, the man's bad breath overpowering her senses.

His eyes were wide, staring, and she wondered how high on drugs her two assailants might be. He stank, as if he hadn't washed in days, his face covered in pustules and a days-old beard.

'Leave her,' said the first man, stepping forward. 'We need to find who she's with.'

The second man tightened his hold on Nina's hair and leaned closer to her.

She whimpered, feeling his hardness against her, and squirmed in his grip.

'Where's your friend?' he said. 'Point.'

Nina remained silent, then cried out as the man shook her, and she bit her lip.

She tasted blood on her tongue, the coppery taste swirling in her mouth. Shaking, she raised her hand and pointed towards the house.

'He went that way,' she whispered, appalled that she couldn't do anything to warn Kyle he was in danger.

The first man stepped forward. 'Bring her with us, Peter. She might be useful.'

'I'm sure she will be.' Her captor leaned closer. 'Very useful.'

His grip loosened on her hair, and Nina hissed between her teeth as she straightened, her back muscles burning.

She rubbed her neck to ease the pain before the man wrapped his fingers round her arm and began to follow his colleague.

'Don't try anything, bitch,' he murmured. 'Don't you be thinking about calling out to your friend.'

Nina slipped in the mud under her feet as he dragged her forward.

'Hurry,' he said, pulling her along.

They caught up with the second man, Peter deferring to his lead.

Nina stumbled over the paddock between the two men, her shoulders slumped, her whole body exhausted.

She chided herself for not being more alert, for not expecting Hudson to have men searching the perimeter for the arsonists that had razed his outbuilding to the ground.

As the first man pushed open the back door, his body stiffened, and she followed his gaze to the exit from the kitchen, where Jock Hudson stood with his hands on his hips, glaring at her.

'Where did you find her?'

'Perimeter. Opposite the back door, sir.'

The second of the men stepped forward. 'We were thinking, sir – she could probably tell us where Kyle is hiding.'

Hudson laughed, stepped to one side, and beckoned to someone out of sight in the passageway.

'No need,' he said, as Larry pushed Kyle into the kitchen, the FBI agent's guns in his hands.

Nina staggered backwards and gasped.

A black eye had begun to bruise the left side of Kyle's face, the socket swollen. Blood seeped from his shoulder, the stab wound open and raw.

Hudson spun back to face Nina, his lip curling as he advanced on her. 'So, this is the truck stop owner's daughter, is it?'

Nina felt heat flush her face as he stepped closer, appraising her. He reached out and ran his hand down her cheek.

Nina fought down bile and kept her gaze trained on the opposite wall, gritting her teeth as his hand moved lower until he was cupping her breast.

'Don't ignore me,' he murmured, his voice sending a chill through her body. 'We're only just getting started.'

He squeezed her breast, and she yelped, jerking her body away from him.

Kyle lurched forward, cursing loudly as two of Hudson's henchmen dragged him back, away from Nina.

Hudson laughed. 'I see. That's how it is, is it?'

He nodded to the smaller man, who stepped forward and punched Kyle in the stomach again.

The FBI agent emitted a pained grunt and collapsed to the floor.

Hudson moved across to the special agent, bending down until his face was level with Kyle's. He reached out and forced his thumb into the bleeding knife wound, twisting the broken skin, until the FBI agent writhed in agony.

He screamed, and Nina closed her eyes, trying to block out the primitive sound.

As his scream ebbed away to a muffled curse, she turned to see a satisfied smile on Hudson's face. He leaned closer to Kyle.

'Listen to me, traitor,' he said. 'Do you know what we're going to do? Do you?' He chuckled. 'Me and the boys are going to have some fun with your woman. And you're going to watch.' He glanced over his shoulder, his eyes gleaming.

Nina staggered, her legs almost giving way, and an uncontrollable shake began in her hands.

Hudson turned back to Kyle. 'Thought you were better than me, didn't you?' His hand shot out, back-handing the special agent across his cheek.

Kyle fell back with the force of the blow, blood spattering across the floor once more.

He steadied himself, then glared at Hudson, working his jaw. Seconds passed, then he spat out a broken tooth.

The older man laughed. 'You'll be losing a few more of those by the time we've finished with you,' he said. 'As well as a few other parts.' He stepped back and signalled to his men. 'Search him,' he said, and crossed his arms over his chest as two of his men brushed past him. 'See what else he's hiding on him.'

The large man held Kyle's arms behind him as they approached him, and Nina cried out as one took a swing at the FBI agent.

Kyle staggered at the blow to his stomach, his breath hissing between his teeth. He slumped over, wheezing until the man holding him hauled him upright, and then the two thugs began to search his clothing.

One of them reached round and pulled Kyle's jacket open, tearing the seams.

The taller of the two glanced over his shoulder at Hudson and raised an eyebrow.

'What have you got?' he asked, and stepped closer.

The man pulled on the lining of the jacket, and the satellite phone fell into his hand.

Nina's eyes opened wide. Kyle gave her an almost imperceptible shake of his head, and she lowered her gaze.

'Satellite phone, eh?' said Hudson, turning the small plastic-covered device in his hand. 'Thinking of calling for back-up, were you?'

His gaze shifted to the smaller man standing next to Kyle, and he nodded.

The man spun on his heel and back-handed the FBI agent hard across his face.

Nina fought down the urge to be sick as the sound of breaking cartilage filled the small space and blood spattered across the floor.

Kyle cursed, then rubbed his face against his shoulder and glared at Hudson, blood trickling from his nose.

'Actually, I figured I could deal with you myself, if this is the best you can do,' he said, staring at each of the men in turn before his glare rested on Hudson.

The older man laughed before he began to cough, a deep wracking noise that consumed his body.

He reached into a pocket and pulled out a handkerchief, put it to his face, and closed his eyes while the choking noises subsided, then removed the cloth and hawked on the floor.

He pushed the handkerchief away and pointed at the smaller man when he spoke.

'Be careful, FBI man. Frank here was a welterweight boxer – quite successful until he got banned for killing an opponent.'

'It was an accident,' said the man, holding his palms upwards.

A ripple of laughter filled the room.

Nina edged backwards, trying to put as much distance between herself and the small crowd of men, her thoughts spinning.

Hudson held up his hand to silence his men, then

dropped the phone to the floor, stepped forward, and drove his heel through the device.

Splinters of plastic and metal spat across the concrete surface.

Kyle shrugged. 'It doesn't matter, Hudson,' he said, wiping his sleeve across his mouth, smearing blood over his face. 'I radioed my team from the Flanagan property over three hours ago. They've got the licence plate of the truck. They'll have the entire resources of the Division and the San Francisco Police Department hunting it.'

He frowned, and Nina stared at Hudson as he began to convulse with laughter.

'Oh, really?' he sneered. 'Is that what you think?' He clicked his fingers, signalling to one of his men in the hallway outside. 'Go and get our other guest.'

Nina tried to remain still, desperate to avoid drawing attention to herself while Kyle and Hudson glared at each other, the seconds ticking past.

Why wasn't Hudson concerned about the truck being intercepted? Was there more to his twisted plans than Kyle had managed to uncover?

Her thoughts were interrupted by a commotion in the hallway, and she stumbled forward as she realized who the second of the voices belonged to. A familiar figure was pushed into the room.

'Jeff?'

She spun away from Ross's father to Hudson, her mouth open in shock, bewildered. 'What's going on?'

Jeff had paled when she'd called out. 'Nina? What are you doing here? Ross was meant to keep you away.'

Nina staggered backwards, and Peter's hand shot out to steady her.

'Keep me away? What do you mean?' She turned to Kyle. 'What the hell is going on around here?'

Hudson's cackle of laughter filled the room, and he clapped his hands. 'Well, isn't this nice?' He beamed. 'A reunion.'

He strolled over to Jeff and slapped him on the back, then pushed him towards Nina. 'Why don't you explain to the lovely Miss O'Brien what you've been up to in her absence, hmm? Bring her up to speed?' He checked his watch, and the mirth left his features. 'Quickly now. You're running out of time.'

Nina noticed how the farmer's hands shook as he used his sleeve to wipe the sweat from his brow, and then rubbed at his eyes before he took a shaking breath.

'Your radio signal didn't get through,' he mumbled, keeping his head bowed, his eyes lowered, staring at the floor.

'What?' Kyle took a step towards the older man before Larry put a restraining hand against his chest, earning a glare from the FBI agent. 'What did you say?'

Jeff sighed. 'I disabled it so your signal wouldn't be strong enough to reach one of the repeater transceivers up on the range,' he said. 'It could only transmit shortwave.'

He lifted his gaze to Nina, pain etched in his eyes. 'It

was picked up by Peter,' he explained, pointing at the man next to her.

'Jeff? What have you done?' Nina covered her mouth in horror.

'So, you see Kyle, my truck is still on schedule.' Hudson grinned indulgently.

'How could you?' Nina demanded. 'I've known you all my life, Jeff – why would you help this madman?'

'You stupid bastard,' hissed Kyle. 'Do you realize how many people you'll help to kill?'

Jeff's hands trembled, and he scratched absently at his earlobe. 'He said he'd kill Tim if I didn't help him,' he mumbled, then stared at Kyle. 'I didn't have a choice.'

'Shit.' The FBI agent's shoulders sagged.

Hudson spat out a laugh. 'Wonderful sob story, Jeff,' he sneered. 'You almost sounded like a victim for a moment there.'

'Please,' said Jeff, his gaze nervously darting to Nina, then back. 'She doesn't need to know.'

'Oh, I think she does,' grinned Hudson. 'You see, Miss O'Brien, your old neighbour here isn't only responsible for the trick with the radio.'

'What the hell do you mean?'

Hudson's eyes gleamed. 'Jeff here has been very good at ensuring our drug operation here has remained undetected for the past year, haven't you?'

Jeff held up his hands in protest. 'I needed the money, Nina! You've seen what the drought has done to the valley – I had no idea he was making a poison as well, I swear!'

'Oh, great,' said Nina sarcastically. 'Drugs are fine, but poison isn't? Suzanne would be ashamed of you,' she snapped. Her heart skipped a beat. 'Oh my God, is Ross involved as well?'

'No.' Kyle spoke, his calm voice cutting through the tension in the room. 'He and Tim had no idea until they stumbled across Hudson's drug operation by accident six months ago.' He looked at Jeff. 'It's kind of ironic that your own sons exposed the same operation that's been keeping your farm going, isn't it?'

'Enough,' snapped Hudson. He snatched Kyle's gun from Larry's hand and pointed it at Jeff. 'You've served your purpose,' he said, and pulled the trigger.

Nina shrieked, shutting her eyes and covering her ears with her hands as the gunshot reverberated off the walls of the kitchen.

Rough hands grabbed her, forcing her to open her eyes so she didn't stumble.

She whimpered at the sight of Ross's father crumpled on the tiled floor, blood pouring from a gaping wound in his chest.

His mouth opened and closed soundlessly, his eyes open wide, until a shudder wracked his body and he lay still.

Nina wiped angrily at the tears in her eyes.

'You bastard,' hissed Kyle.

Hudson's head jerked round until he was glaring directly at Kyle.

'Now no-one will come and rescue you,' he snarled.

He raised himself up to his full height and turned to Larry.

'How much longer?'

'Twenty minutes, max. Once the charges are laid, we'll clear out. Make sure we're out of here before they blow.'

'You'll never make it,' Kyle wheezed, bending over. 'The creek is flooded going west, and there's a landslide blocking the highway through the mountains. You're trapped.'

Nina watched as a look of disbelief crossed Hudson's face.

A deep chuckle shook his shoulders before he couldn't contain himself anymore, and a raucous laughter rocked the confines of the small room.

His men joined in, leering at Nina and throwing abuse towards Kyle.

Hudson gained control of his laughter and raised his hand, the noise level dropping to a murmur.

'See, Kyle, I had my suspicions about you,' he said, waggling his finger at the special agent as he paced in front of him. 'Which is why I decided you weren't going to know about the *whole* plan.' Hudson shivered. 'When that poison gets released during the commuter rush later this morning, I'm going to make sure I'm miles away.'

'Coward.' The words left Nina's lips before she could stop them, her fury erupting.

Kyle's eyes flashed in warning, and she took a step backwards as Hudson spun round to face her.

'What did you say?'

Nina was saved from having to respond as Hudson's attention was drawn towards movement at the door.

'Where the hell have you two been?' he spat.

THIRTY-FOUR

Nina's skin prickled at the sight of the diminutive blonde, anger still surging through her body.

'Cleaning up,' said Dani, and flicked her freshly washed hair over her shoulder. 'It's disgusting out there.' She finished fluffing her hair and looked at Nina, a cold stare that appraised the younger woman and made her look away. 'Running out on your friend, were you?'

Nina bit her lip and tried to ignore the hot sting in her eyes.

Sean entered the room, his clothes clean. He sneered at Nina. 'Well, well, well,' he said. 'Guess your little plan to escape failed, then?'

Nina's head shot up, and she opened her mouth to speak before Kyle coughed and shot her a warning look. She clenched her fists, her jagged nails digging into her palms.

'I told you to make sure he was dead,' said Hudson, pointing at Kyle, his face close to Dani's. 'Which part of that order didn't you understand?'

Dani shrugged, a petulant expression on her face.

'They escaped,' she said. 'We nearly caught up with them by the creek, but they'd disappeared by the time we got there.'

'They're here now, Hudson,' said Sean. 'At least we can deal with them here.'

Hudson snorted. 'Are there any more loose ends you want to tell me about?' He spun round to face Sean. 'Well?'

Sean cleared his throat and glanced at Dani. 'There was a man – at the truck stop. I shot him – got him in the leg, as well as a gut shot.' He shrugged. 'We didn't have any spare ammunition, so we figured he'd die anyway.'

Nina tried to fight down the panic rising in her. When they'd left Ross, the only injury he'd sustained was the gunshot wound to his leg.

'W-what?' she managed. 'I thought he was just shot in the leg?'

Dani swung round to face her. 'Maybe if you'd stuck around to help him instead of running with your tail between your legs, he wouldn't have been shot trying to save you,' she said, and shrugged her shoulders.

Nina struggled against the hands that held her.

Hudson ignored her, and paced the floor, rubbing his chin with his hand.

'Who was he?' he asked. 'Anyone on our radar?'

'I think he was your neighbour's older son,' Sean replied. 'He didn't recognize me, but I'd seen him a couple of months ago when we were out this way.'

Hudson stopped pacing, turned to Larry, and held out his hand. 'Give me one of those.'

Larry grinned and handed him a gun. Hudson checked it and handed it to Sean.

'Take this. Go back to the truck stop. Make sure he's dead this time.'

'No!' Nina screamed. Her gaze darted between the two men. 'You can't do that!'

'I can go back,' said Dani, ignoring her and stepping forward to take the weapon.

'No.' Hudson put out his arm to stop her. 'Sean goes.' An evil grin split his mouth open. 'He needs the target practice.'

'True.' Dani joined in his laughter.

Hudson turned back to Sean. 'Why are you still here?'

Nina glared at him as Sean left the room. 'Please, don't make him do it,' she pleaded.

A smile curled his lips. 'I'll do whatever I like,' he said. 'I don't think you're in a position to negotiate, do you?'

Dani moved closer to Hudson, an eager look in her eyes. 'What do you want me to do? I could take care of her.'

Her hand slipped to the gun strapped to her hip, and in

265

one smooth movement she had it pointed in Nina's face, her finger covering the trigger.

Hudson rubbed his chin and looked sideways at Nina. 'Yes,' he mused. 'We still need to deal with this member of the O'Brien family.' He cursed. 'I thought getting rid of her father would solve the problem of us being watched.'

Nina blinked. 'What do you mean, "getting rid of" my father?'

Dani laughed and lowered the gun a little, although she still kept it trained on Nina's chest.

'Dani here is an exceptional actress,' said Hudson, 'as well as having the dubious honour of being the most cold-blooded killer I've ever known.'

Nina looked from one to the other, confused.

'What he means,' said Dani, once she stopped laughing, 'is that it would have attracted too much attention if I'd simply shot your father to get him out of our way.'

'What?' Nina looked across the room to Kyle, who was trying to avoid her gaze.

'Instead, we had to make sure he left of his own accord,' Dani continued. 'Or make it look like he was too incompetent to run his own business.'

Nina's jaw dropped open as the implications of Dani's words sunk in.

'Y-you mean, he's not sick?'

'Homesick, maybe,' said Dani, grinning.

Nina stepped back, stumbled against the man that held her, and gasped, 'You bitch.'

Dani cackled. 'Thank you,' she said, and executed a small bow. 'I aim to please.'

Hudson smiled. 'Like I said – cold-blooded.' He leaned forward and used the palm of his hand to lower Dani's arm before he stepped in front of Nina.

'Dani here has been *very* busy the past month getting to know your father's business,' he crowed. 'Little things went missing to start off with, just to make him feel forgetful.' His face darkened. 'Then she put the pressure on. People started talking in town about how Clint O'Brien was getting confused. Making mistakes.'

Nina groaned. She recalled the phone calls from local businesses – when her father couldn't remember where he'd parked his car, only to find it two blocks over from where he insisted he'd left it, or opening the truck stop late in the morning because all the clocks in the building were running an hour late.

'You did all that?' she whispered.

Dani nodded, a gleam in her eyes.

'But the accident,' said Nina. 'With the fuel tanks. That was you too?'

A smile spread across the other woman's face.

'You *bitch*.'

Nina broke free from her captors' hold, and launched herself across the room, both hands raised, ready to throttle the woman.

'No!'

Kyle yelled as Dani's arm swept upwards, the gun drawing level with Nina's forehead.

Hudson moved fast, his hand knocking Dani's arm as the gun went off, the bullet lodging in the wall behind Nina.

He pivoted and slapped Nina across the face, and she cried out, falling to the floor before he reached down, hauled her to her feet, and shook her.

'It's about time I dealt with you,' he hissed.

THIRTY-FIVE

Ross opened his eyes, the coughing fit waking him.

He blinked, wondering why he was lying on a hard concrete floor, a cold wind blowing through an open door, the rain reduced to a steady drizzle, before he remembered.

He cried out when he rolled onto his side, his weight falling on his injured leg.

Fighting the urge to black out again, he checked his watch and tried to work out how long he'd been unconscious.

He concentrated on taking deep breaths, working through the pain that consumed him, and carefully raised himself up into a sitting position.

A trail of blood covered the floor from the door to where he sat, and he recalled dragging himself across the forecourt into the shelter of the building.

After that, his mind was a blank.

Until now.

He hissed through his teeth as another bolt of pain shot up his leg, and tried to focus on breathing.

Sweat poured from his brow despite the cold. He removed the bloodied jacket lining and checked his leg. To his relief, the blood appeared to have clotted. He shrugged his t-shirt off his back, tore it into strips, and tied lengths of it around the wound to stop it reopening.

Satisfied, he turned his attention to the public phone on the wall, Nina's cell phone perched on top of it, tantalisingly close.

His vision blurred, the room spinning, before he shook his head and closed his eyes, desperately trying to avoid the blackness that sought him out, dragging him into unconsciousness.

He cried out as a spasm shook his leg, then gritted his teeth, opened his eyes, and began to drag his body towards the phone.

As he hauled his weight across the floor, he whimpered at each movement.

Reaching the wall, he paused, panting from the effort.

He stretched up his arm, his fingers brushing the plastic casing of the landline, the cell phone on top of it still out of reach.

'Shit!'

He waited until the pain subsided enough that he could shuffle round and sit with his back to the wall, his legs splayed out in front of him.

The broom Phil had used to sweep up the glass earlier that night was only inches away from his good leg, propped against the counter, and he stretched until his toes met the soft nylon bristles.

He kicked out and then cursed as the broom wobbled but failed to fall over.

Inching forward, he leaned back on his palms until his foot found the broom once more, and kicked.

The broom moved, its handle sliding along the counter, and then began to fall towards him.

He cried out as he tumbled sideways to catch it, moving his injured leg as his fingers wrapped around the handle.

Sweat poured down his face, and his eyesight began to blacken at the edges. Ross fought down the urge to faint and instead hefted the broom in his hands and aimed it at the telephone receiver.

With one swift jab, it fell from its cradle, and swung in the air above Ross's head on a coiled cable.

He grinned, reached up to grab it, and put it to his ear.

Silence filled the line.

Ross dropped the receiver, letting it swing against the wall, and then his attention snapped back to the cell phone.

Another jab with the broom handle sent it toppling towards the floor, and he reached out with his hands seconds before it met the hard surface.

Exhausted, he shoved the broom aside and held up the phone.

A weak signal icon hovered at the top of the screen, and he exhaled with relief. He dialled nine-one-one and nearly cried out when a dispatcher answered within seconds.

'My name's Ross Flanagan,' he began in a shaking voice. 'I'm at the Mistake Creek Truck Stop. I've been shot.'

The purr of an approaching vehicle reached his ears.

He frowned. 'Hang on a minute.'

His heart pounding, he held his breath as powerful headlights swept across the forecourt.

A door opened, and a familiar figure climbed out and stood in front of the car, silhouetted against its frame.

'Oh shit.'

Ross clutched the cell phone to his chest, ignoring the urgent tones of the dispatcher at the other end of the line. He leaned over and grasped hold of the broom, then began to haul himself away from the wall, trying to put as much distance as possible between himself and the open doorway.

He gritted his teeth as pain coursed through his body, tremors seizing his limbs.

Footsteps sloshed through the puddles on the forecourt, getting closer.

Ross pulled the broom along the floor with him, in a desperate hope that Sean would be unarmed, that he'd be able to defend himself.

He gritted his teeth as another spasm shook his body,

the cell phone slipping through his fingers and skidding across the floor away from him.

He checked over his shoulder as he crawled and tried in vain to push the thought from his mind that this could be the end, that he could die within seconds.

He froze as the footsteps stopped on the threshold. The beam from a flashlight swept across the floor, tracking the smeared blood stains.

'Not a lot of use in hiding, Ross,' Sean called. 'You've left one hell of a trail of breadcrumbs.'

His footsteps echoed off the walls, and Ross's eyes widened as the beam from the flashlight drew closer.

He dropped the broom and fumbled in the darkness, his fingers scratching at the floor, seeking something they couldn't find.

He crawled forwards again, sobbing as the pain consumed him, his fingers grasping nothing but air, until—

'Hold it right there.'

Ross froze.

Sean towered over him, his gun raised, his finger on the trigger. He kicked the discarded broom at Ross's feet and chuckled.

'You really didn't think you were going to try and kill me with this, did you?'

'No,' said Ross. 'I didn't.'

He rolled onto his back, the nail-gun between his hands with the safety guard pulled back, and fired.

THIRTY-SIX

Nina stopped listening to Hudson and instead concentrated on a low pulse she could hear in the distance, coming closer.

It sounded familiar, a mechanical throb that approached the property at speed.

Hudson heard it too and stopped pacing, his head cocked to one side. A smile formed across his lips, and he looked at his men.

'The helicopter's almost here. Get ready to start loading it.'

Nina slumped in her captor's arms.

A helicopter explained why Hudson wasn't concerned that the creek was flooded, or that a landslide had blocked the highway through the hills.

He'd never had any intention to leave by road.

Kyle cursed loudly, and she turned to him, seeing the

look of desperation that flitted across his face before he recovered and listened to Hudson giving orders to his men.

Their gaze locked, he shook his head, and she knew then that he had no plan. No way to escape.

Larry stepped forward, ignoring Dani who stood with one hand on her hip, glaring at Nina.

'Boss, I've got a better idea what to do with these two.'

'What?'

'Why don't I put them in the basement with the boy?'

Dani threw her hands up in disgust.

Larry ignored her and kept talking. 'There'd be no evidence of them ever being here.'

'If you're going to do that, I may as well shoot them first,' said Dani.

Hudson scratched his chin. 'But that would be over too quickly for my liking,' he said, and turned to Larry. 'Do it – but put them in a different room from the farmer's boy.'

Larry nodded and motioned for the two men who held Kyle to follow him as he pushed Nina from the room and along the passageway towards the back of the house.

'You can't do this!' Nina pleaded. 'Can't you see he's lost his mind?'

'Shut up. Keep walking.'

Larry opened a door at the end of the passageway and flipped a light switch.

A flight of stairs led down into the gloom.

Nina tried to break past her captor, but he was too quick. Seizing her by the arm, he pulled her down the stairs, the sound of Kyle struggling between the other two men reaching her ears.

At the bottom of the stairs, Larry turned right, passing several closed doors, solid bolts in place on each.

Nina trembled, wondering who else Hudson held captive, then shouted,

'Tim! Are you here?'

A subdued voice emanated from behind one of the doors, and Nina choked back a sob.

'He's only nineteen!' she yelled. 'Let him go – please!'

Larry's hand snaked across her mouth, muffling her cries.

Her mind raced as she questioned every single choice she'd made the past four weeks. If only she'd listened to her father's arguments that there was nothing wrong with him. If only she hadn't insisted on returning to Mistake Creek, hell-bent on selling the truck stop.

And if only Ross hadn't insisted on being his usual generous self and helping her, he'd have been home, protecting his family tonight, and not her.

Tears began to course down her cheeks as Larry paused in front of the last door.

He shot the bolt back, then stepped aside and shoved Nina into the small room, Kyle stumbling after her, scowling at the two men who had held him.

The smaller of the two reached out to turn the light off, but Larry stopped him.

'No,' he said, turning to Nina and Kyle. 'Let them

watch what happens when they don't mind their own business.'

The men laughed and backed out of the makeshift cell.

Larry pulled the door, began to close it, and then glanced at Kyle over his shoulder.

'Look on the bright side. At least it'll be a short stay.'

As soon as the door slammed shut and the bolts slid across its outer surface, Kyle leapt from his sitting position and made his way towards the charge that had been attached to the wall.

Nina crossed the room to join him, peering round his body to see what he was doing.

His hands moved cautiously over the surface of the outer casing, his face a mask of concentration. He dropped to a crouch and craned his neck to one side so he could see underneath the box-like appendage.

Nina followed the path of his hands with her eyes as he tested and prodded the plastic cover. A red light blinked on the upper surface, and wires protruded from the left-hand side nearest the door.

Eventually he straightened, and looked down at her, his jaw set.

'I can't disarm it.'

'What?' Nina's eyes opened wide. 'But you have to – there has to be some way!'

'I can't,' he said. 'There's no way. There's an anti-tamper mechanism fixed to it. If I try to disarm it, it's going to explode anyway. And they've set it up so it's triggered remotely, not by a timer from here.'

'Why?'

Kyle checked over his shoulder at the blinking light. 'I guess so they could make sure they were all clear before it goes off.'

A sob escaped Nina's lips. 'We're going to die, aren't we?'

'I'm sorry,' said Kyle, pulling her into his arms. 'I'm so sorry.'

Nina sniffed and wiped her eyes. She returned Kyle's embrace, a desperate need for human contact. 'This can't be happening.'

Kyle smoothed her hair, his breath caressing her ear. He said nothing and simply listened, letting her talk.

'I can't believe they've killed Ross,' she wept, curling her fingers into his shirt. 'He's such a good man – he was just trying to help us.'

'I hate this job sometimes.'

Nina raised her head and met his gaze. 'Just sometimes?'

'Yeah. Especially the part where innocent people like you get sucked into the mess I'm supposed to be fixing.'

'You did your best, Kyle. Hopefully your boss will find the truck in time, somehow.'

'Maybe.'

Nina peered around the room, her gaze falling to the blinking red light of the charge set onto the wall.

'Will it be quick?'

She heard him swallow.

'I hope so,' he whispered. 'I've never been blown up before, so I don't know.'

Nina smiled through her tears, despite the dire situation. 'How do you do that, Kyle? How can you joke about it?'

'It's the only way I know how to cope.'

They fell silent, each lost in their own thoughts.

Nina closed her eyes. Twelve hours ago, her only concern was whether the storm would tear apart the truck stop. She sniffed, and Kyle's arms tightened around her.

His lips brushed her hair before he rested his cheek against her forehead, his hands caressing her shoulders, soothing her.

Without warning, the floor and walls shook violently, sending plaster dust over Nina and Kyle as they lurched and stumbled, trying to keep their balance.

Nina screamed, terrified, as ceiling panels fell to the floor, exposing wires and timber supports.

'Over here!' yelled Kyle, and pulled her with him to the door, seeking shelter from the debris tumbling around them.

Nina pulled her shirt up, covering her mouth and nose, and as the tremors subsided, she leaned against the wall, her legs shaking.

'They're destroying the house,' she gasped.

Kyle shook his head. 'That was one of the outbuildings,' he said.

Nina glanced over her shoulder to where the charge continued to blink.

'We're going to be buried alive before that goes off,' she said, her voice trembling. 'Aren't we?'

He ran a hand through his hair, white powder dusting his shoulders. 'I don't know,' he said, his face solemn. 'It depends on where they've placed the charges, what sort of explosives they're using…'

Nina held her hand up to stop him. 'I don't want to know the rest.'

A second explosion pushed her off balance, sending her flying into Kyle.

He swore as they collapsed to the floor, and she realized he'd fallen on his wounded shoulder.

'Take cover,' he yelled, and at the same time ducked his head between his knees, his forearms crossing the back of his skull.

Nina copied him, an ominous creaking sound reaching her ears before the ceiling panel above them collapsed.

She whimpered in terror as the low wattage light bulb swung back and forth, the pressure wave sweeping through the basement, the thought of enduring the final, fatal, explosion in darkness too much to bear.

As the noise subsided, she raised her head.

Kyle had sat upright, frowning at the door.

Nina waited for the ringing in her ears to ease, then heard it too.

Footsteps, hurrying along the passageway outside. Heading towards them.

'Give me your boots,' Kyle said under his breath.

'What?'

'Your boots. Now!'

Nina leaned down, unlaced her boots, then slipped them off and handed them to Kyle.

He snatched them from her, hurried to the pile of fallen ceiling panels, and tucked her boots under them, only the toes protruding. He stepped back, reached down to adjust one of the panels, then jogged back to the door and checked his handiwork.

He motioned to Nina to join him next to the wall, and then put a finger to his lips.

She nodded, cleared the distance between them in four long strides, and cowered behind him, her back to the charge.

Kyle moved beside her, bent down, and picked up half of a broken timber beam that had fallen from the ceiling cavity, hefting it in his grip, testing its weight.

As the footsteps stopped outside the door, they heard a man curse before the bolt was released.

The door swung inwards, hiding them from sight.

A cough and then another curse preceded a flashlight beam being swung around the room, sweeping back and forth over the devastation in the dusty gloom.

'Ah, fuck.'

The profanity escaped from the man as the flashlight found the boots lying under the debris in the shadows.

Larry stepped forward, and Kyle pounced, shoving the door shut and swinging the length of timber down onto the base of the man's neck.

He grunted in surprise, but the timber was already too warped and broken to cause any lasting damage. He spun, his eyes opening wide, before he held his hand up to ward off another blow to his head.

'Stop!' he bellowed. 'I'm here to help you!'

THIRTY-SEVEN

Kyle raised the makeshift weapon above his head, ready to strike.

'Explain,' he said.

Larry stepped back, his hand still raised. 'I'm DEA agent Lawrence Whitman,' he said. 'I've been deep cover in Hudson's crew for the past twelve months.'

Nina covered her mouth in shock as Kyle's eyes narrowed.

'Prove it,' he said.

Larry pointed to the ceiling. 'I set the charges to go off early,' he said. 'Right now, half of Hudson's men are dead.' He flicked his wrist and checked his watch. 'In precisely sixty seconds, the first of the charges in the house you're under will go off. If you don't want to be buried alive, I'd suggest you come with me.'

'I'll go with that,' said Kyle, and pushed Nina towards the door.

Her hand was crushed in Larry's as he pulled her along the passageway, Kyle's footsteps close behind.

'Wait,' he shouted.

Larry stopped.

Kyle had paused next to a door.

'Ross's brother is in here,' he said. He spoke to Larry, but his gaze remained on Nina as he spoke. 'Get her out of here. I'll be right behind.'

'I'll help you.' Nina lurched forward.

'No.' He held up his hand. 'Enough, Nina. Too many people have died already tonight. I'm not letting them take you.'

He turned to Larry. 'Get out of here – fast.'

Nina thought her shoulder would be ripped from its socket as Larry spun round and started running down the length of the passageway, putting as much distance as he could between them and the explosive charge.

She tried to stop him, to explain they had to wait for Kyle and Ross's brother to catch up with them, that they couldn't leave them behind, but the special agent kept running, refusing to slow.

'We've got to get out of here,' he yelled. 'When someone says "go" in this job, they mean it.'

Nina gritted her teeth and concentrated on running. She wondered how many explosives had been laid throughout the building and how far away they'd need to be to escape the onslaught.

How much time did they have?

A loud *boom* from outside shook the walls, sending plaster tumbling from the ceiling and walls around them.

Nina cried out as part of the structure crumbled, sending a shower of debris over her head. She stumbled, and her leg caught on something that tripped her, then wrapped around her calf muscle and pulled.

She looked down and screamed.

Dani had crawled through the smoke and flames, her face bloodied from the fallen masonry, one leg bent backwards at an impossible angle. She glared up at Nina, a manic gleam in her eyes.

'You're mine,' she hissed, a split second before her gaze snapped sideways.

'No she's not,' said Larry, appearing at Nina's side, and aimed his gun.

Dani's eyes widened, and then the bullet hit her square in the forehead, and she jerked backwards, dead before she hit the floor.

Nina gulped, fighting down the urge to be sick, and stepped back quickly, the dead woman's fingers sliding from her leg.

Repulsed, she covered her mouth with her hand before Larry grabbed her arm.

'We're not out of danger yet,' he urged.

'Hang on.' She stopped, jerking Larry to a standstill, and wiped the plaster dust from her eyes.

'Are you okay?'

'Yes.'

'Then don't slow down!'

He tugged her arm and pulled her back into a run.

Nina swallowed the argument that threatened to burst from her lips and instead forced another burst of energy from her aching legs.

As they reached a corner that angled round to the right, Nina risked a glance over her shoulder.

There was no sign of Kyle or Tim.

She turned her attention back to Larry as a loud curse emanated from him. He slid to a halt, and she careened into him.

'Stand back and cover your ears.'

She did as he commanded, her eyes widening as he handed her his gun. He removed a large calibre pistol from the waistband of his jeans and aimed it at the locked door in front of them.

He winked at her, a manic expression crossing his face, and then angled his head away from the blast zone, closed his eyes, and pulled the trigger.

Even with her fingers in her ears, Nina's body shook from the explosive force.

The door splintered, the metal parts of the locking mechanism spinning across the floor before Larry began to kick at the remaining woodwork and then beckoned to her.

'Get out. Now. I'll be right behind you.'

Nina scrambled through the narrow opening. Before she'd stepped clear, the special agent was already on her heels.

He grunted as he forced his body through the small gap, then grabbed her wrist and pulled.

'Move.'

Nina stumbled after him, glancing left and right at the sheer devastation around them.

Two of the outbuildings were on fire, accounting for the explosions they'd heard while still trapped inside the main house.

The shed she and Kyle had destroyed smouldered to her left, the rain having dampened the flames.

She forced a burst of speed and drew alongside Larry.

'Where are we headed?'

'That tree line over there,' he said through gritted teeth. 'If we can make it.'

A third explosion rocked the earth, closer this time, which sent them diving to the ground for cover.

Nina peered over her shoulder as the initial noise died down.

A crater had appeared where the machine shed had once stood. Now, a fire pit of twisted metal replaced the structure, the stink of burning fuel and plastic filling the air with a noxious black smoke.

Larry was already on his feet, reaching down to her. 'Come on. The house is next.'

'But…'

'Nina, now!'

She scrambled to her feet, exhausted, but realising how much danger they were both in, she followed Larry towards the trees at the edge of the property line.

She held her arm across her nose and mouth, breathing through the smoke and fumes that wafted across the landscape around them.

She copied Larry as they reached the trees and dropped to the ground. She hoped the branches above would lessen the impact of any falling debris.

Larry pushed her head down as, one by one, the gas tanks exploded and shot jagged metal and flames skywards.

Nina whimpered as large pieces of metal flew into the trees around them.

A loud *whack* cut through the noise, and Larry cursed.

'That was close.'

Nina twisted her neck and looked at him, then glimpsed the shard of metal sticking out of the tree trunk next to his head.

'Stay still,' he said. 'That wasn't the last one.'

Nina closed her eyes and lowered her head to her arms, hoping neither of them would be decapitated.

Sure enough, the final gas tank exploded with an enormous *whump*, and the branches above them shook as shrapnel flew into the trees.

When the noise died away, Nina raised her head and glanced at Larry beside her.

He had raised himself up on his elbows and was staring, jaw clenched, at the direction from which they'd fled.

Nina eased into a crouching position to see what he was looking at and then cried out, her hand covering her mouth.

The house had been completely destroyed, fallen masonry and household items littering the area.

Nina stared from one side to the other, her mouth open in shock at the devastation before them.

The house had been cleaved in half. To her left lay the remains of a dining table, its surface split in two. On her right, a whole wall had collapsed, flames licking at the fallen roof beams that lay split and torn.

A jagged line stretched through the middle of the remains of the building, the path of the explosive charges laid bare for all to see.

Nina sank back onto her heels, her hands dropping to her lap, shaking.

She squinted, peering into the flames, desperately looking for movement, for signs of life.

A roof beam creaked, then exploded in a shower of sparks and tumbled to the ground, sending up a flash of flames and smoke.

No shadows moved. No-one emerged from the smoke.

Larry joined her and placed a hand on her shoulder before squatting next to her. 'I'm sorry, Nina. He would've done all he could.'

She nodded, unable to form the words that clouded her thoughts.

THIRTY-EIGHT

'Get down!'

Nina dived for cover as Larry dropped to the ground next to her.

A helicopter swept low over the treeline, the wash from its rotor blades flattening the undergrowth and saplings above Nina's head.

'Shit!'

'I wondered where he was hiding.' Larry leapt into a crouch, shielding his eyes from the detritus that flew in the air around him. 'Stay here.'

'Where are you going?'

Larry pointed at the helicopter. 'That's Hudson's escape plan,' he shouted over the noise of the helicopter. 'He was never going with the rest of his men – I have to stop him!'

'How?'

A grin spread across his face, and Nina noticed the same look in his eyes as she'd seen in Kyle's only hours before.

'I've got a present for him,' he said, patted her shoulder, and then ran through the tree line and back towards the ruins of the machine shed.

Nina crawled until she could peer through the undergrowth and see what he was doing.

Hudson appeared from the side of the ruined house clutching his right leg, his face blackened and his short white hair singed at the edges. Blood ran from a cut above his eyebrow.

He waved frantically at the helicopter and then pointed to a clearing at the far end of the paddock, made sure the pilot followed his instructions, then limped to meet it.

'He's getting away, Larry,' murmured Nina. 'Whatever it is you're going to do, you need to hurry.'

The pilot landed the aircraft without incident, and she watched, frustrated, as Hudson moved towards it.

As Hudson began to climb into the aircraft, a shout from the obliterated barn caught Nina's attention.

Hudson appeared to notice too, turning his head towards the sound.

One of the men that had captured Nina, the younger one they called Peter, staggered across the paddock, his face bloody and burned. He cried out again, holding up his hand to wave at Hudson, and tried to move faster.

292

Nina watched as Hudson spoke with the pilot, who handed the older man an object.

'Oh no,' she whispered, covering her face as she realized what he was going to do.

A single shot rang out in the grey dawn beginning to crest the horizon, echoing around the paddock.

Nina opened her eyes.

Peter's body lay prone in the mud, unmoving, while Hudson climbed into the helicopter and fastened his seatbelt.

As the rotor blades began to spin faster, Nina stood and moved forward, wondering where Larry was.

'Come on,' she muttered. 'He's getting away.'

She sensed movement near the burned-out machine shed, next to one of the old rusting tractors.

Larry appeared, a long thick tube slung over one shoulder.

'Oh my God.' Nina's eyes opened wide. She'd seen what he was carrying on the news coverage of wars in foreign lands – never in California. 'Where the hell did he hide that?'

The helicopter lifted from the ground, its tail rotor nearest to Larry, the pilot oblivious to the danger he was in.

Nina's gaze moved between the helicopter and Larry, wondering why he was waiting, and whether it was possible to miss with one of those things.

As the helicopter continued to rise, Larry remained still, tracking its movement with the weapon.

When the helicopter was level with the treeline, it began to move away from Larry.

Still the DEA agent remained immobile, his feet planted shoulder-width apart.

Nina spotted movement in the cockpit of the aircraft.

As the helicopter had turned, Hudson's line of sight over his property changed and, with it, he had full view of the large man standing in his paddock aiming a rocket-propelled grenade launcher at him.

He began to wave his hands, turned away to speak to the pilot next to him, then turned back to face the sight below him.

A flash from the muzzle of the grenade launcher preceded a fiery smoking trail that arced towards the aircraft.

Nina watched as Larry threw himself to the ground and covered his head, then took the hint and copied the manoeuvre.

As the helicopter exploded in the sky above her, the air seemed to shake, heat and debris surging across the paddock.

The blast subsided quickly, and Nina raised her head in time to watch the burning wreckage fall from the air, a lump of twisted molten metal that shook the ground on impact.

She pushed into a crouch and then stood, a smile on her face as Larry ran towards her.

'That was brilliant!' she shouted as he neared.

He didn't slow down.

Instead, he grabbed her hand and pulled her along with him, away from the crash site.

'No time to celebrate!'

'What? Why?'

'Fuel tanks.'

'Oh shit!'

Nina forced another spurt of energy to keep up with him.

'Over there – behind that truck!'

They slid next to the vehicle, panting.

A second later, a loud *crump* filled the air, and the stench of burning fuel wafted on the breeze.

Larry began to chuckle next to her, and Nina shook her head, amazed.

'Where the hell did you hide that thing?'

Larry rested his head against the vehicle. 'I buried it next to one of the old tractors, when I first got here twelve months ago. Took a bit of organising, but we did it. No-one ever went near the old farm machinery, so I figured it wouldn't be found. I thought it might come in useful one day.'

Nina snorted. 'It certainly did.'

'Did you see his face? I don't think he could believe what was going to happen.'

Nina couldn't keep the bitterness from her voice. 'Serves him right.'

Larry held up his hand to silence her, and she realized that sirens were drawing closer.

She frowned. 'Police?'

'Stay here.'

Larry stood and began to jog towards the track that led from the property to the main road.

Nina watched as one police cruiser and then another swept up the driveway and slid to a stop next to the federal agent.

The police officers leapt from their vehicles, weapons drawn, and placed themselves in a defensive position, shouting orders until Larry held up his hands and knelt on the ground.

Nina began to run as the police advanced on him.

'Stop!' she yelled. 'He's a federal agent!'

She stumbled to a halt as all four officers swung round and aimed their service revolvers at her.

'Put your hands in the air!'

Nina raised her hands. 'Please – listen to me! He's a DEA agent. He knows Kyle Roberts with the FBI. They're trying to stop a poison being released. You have to help us!'

She fell silent as one of the four officers lowered his weapon and walked towards her.

His three colleagues kept their weapons raised, two at Larry, one at her.

Nina's legs were shaking from fatigue and fear, but as the police officer drew closer, she held her chin up defiantly and stared him in the eye.

He stopped a few paces from her.

'State your name for the record, Ma'am.'

'Nina O'Brien.'

'Address?'

'Mistake Creek Truck Stop.' She frowned as the officer's shoulders relaxed slightly, and he lowered his gun. 'What? What is it?'

'Ma'am, we received a phone call from Mistake Creek Truck Stop sixty minutes ago, from Ross Flanagan,' he said. He leaned forward and caught Nina by the arm as she stumbled.

'He asked us to let you know he's alive.'

THIRTY-NINE

Nina sat inside the ambulance, her legs swinging over the edge of the rear fender as the paramedic moved the beam from a small flashlight across her eyes.

His brow creased at the impatient sigh that escaped her lips, and he lowered the flashlight and glared at her.

'Keep still. I'm trying to find out if you're concussed.'

'I was keeping still. You've been pointing that thing in my face for the past two minutes. I think we can safely say I haven't got a concussion.'

He ignored her complaints, put down the flashlight, then wiggled the ends of a stethoscope into his ears and motioned for her to turn around.

'Lift up your shirt for me.'

Nina bunched the material up under her armpits, flinching when the cold surface of the stethoscope touched her skin.

'Deep breaths please.'

She began to breathe in and out through her mouth and tried to ignore the tightness in her lungs as the paramedic moved the small silver disc over her shoulders and rib cage.

He tugged her shirt down for her when he was done.

'You've got some fluid on your lungs. You're asthmatic, right?'

'Yes.'

'When was the last time you had an attack?'

'About six hours ago, I think.'

'Take anything for it?'

'No,' she said. 'My inhaler's still at the truck stop.'

He leaned past her, reached into a box and extracted a plastic case, and handed it to her.

'Keep that one. Just in case.'

'Thanks.' She put it on the floor next to her. 'How did you get past the landslide and floods? Have the roads been cleared?'

'No,' said the paramedic. 'They're still waiting for the water levels to go down. The police organized a dozer to carve enough dirt from the landslide to get our vehicles through, but the road won't be open for days. Have you got somewhere to stay?'

Nina frowned. 'I'm not sure. I think my home is currently being treated as a murder scene.'

The paramedic's eyes opened wider. 'Oh.' He dropped the stethoscope into a box, then wrapped a

Velcro strap around her arm and began to take her blood pressure.

'How long is this going to take?'

'I need to make sure you're going to be okay before I release you,' he said. 'The last thing we want is you thinking you're fine and then collapsing in a few hours' time.'

'I'm just tired.'

'We'll see.' He peered at the digital display on the machine next to him and grunted. 'Right, let's get those cuts and bruises cleaned up.'

Nina jerked her head away as the sting from the first swab of antiseptic fluid swept across her cheek.

The paramedic glared at her, then held her head still with one hand and continued to dab at her face with the other.

'I've dealt with children who've been easier to treat than you,' he grumbled.

'I'm sorry. I just want to find out what's going on around here.'

'I know. So let me do my job. The sooner I can give you the okay, the sooner you can leave.'

'Fine.'

She hissed through her teeth as the paramedic used a fresh swab to clean a cut above her eyebrow.

'Hold on. Nearly done,' he said. 'You're lucky. None of these are going to need stitches.'

'Great.'

Nina couldn't share his enthusiasm. She waited until he reached across the ambulance for more antiseptic lotion and peered over his shoulder.

Larry was talking to the senior police officer, and they both looked up at the sound of another helicopter approaching.

Nina's heart lurched as the aircraft gently dropped out of the sky and landed behind the ruins of the farm property, then relaxed once the doors opened and six dark-clothed men moved swiftly from the helicopter towards the police.

Federal agents.

The paramedic looked over his shoulder. 'Ah. Looks like the cavalry are here,' he said before he turned his attention back to her. 'Okay, last one.'

'Have you heard anything about Kyle Roberts or Tim Flanagan? Has anyone seen them?'

'I'm sorry – I don't know. My orders are to get you cleaned up before the FBI talk to you.'

Nina moved her gaze to the left of the landing area and noticed more red and blue flashing lights.

She frowned. 'Are there more emergency vehicles here?'

'Yeah. The road was blocked round to this side, so they're assisting on the other side of the property. Going to be a long day, I reckon.'

Nina turned her focus back to the paramedic as he finally lowered his hands and smiled at her.

'Right, Miss O'Brien, we're all done here. Just make sure you see a doctor and get some antibiotics so those cuts don't get infected, and you should be fine,' he said, putting his hand on her shoulder.

'Thanks.'

Movement to her right caught her attention, and her mouth dropped open.

'Kyle!'

Nina brushed away the hand of the paramedic, slid from the floor of the ambulance, and rushed to greet the special agent.

He pulled her into a hug, and relief surged through her body.

She couldn't speak for a moment and clung to him, afraid he'd disappear if she let go.

He smoothed her hair, waiting until she was ready to speak.

'I thought you'd been killed,' she whispered.

He chuckled, the sound resonating through his chest against her cheek. 'Not quite.'

'How did you escape?'

'I found a back door,' he grinned.

'Tim?'

'He's fine – he's over on the other side of the wreckage. There's a police officer taking his statement.'

He pulled away, keeping his hands on her shoulders as he ran a critical eye down her body. 'Are you okay?'

She nodded. 'A few cuts and bruises, but I'm fine –

really,' she added when he began to fuss. 'What happens now? Where's the truck?'

'Turns out Larry found out Hudson had intercepted our radio message. He managed to get a call through to his own people in time – the truck was apprehended on the outskirts of the city,' explained Kyle, relief in his eyes. He jerked his head towards the sleek black helicopter. 'I need to go. I have to be back at the office when they debrief the driver and his accomplices.' He managed a smile. 'I think I'm in for a long day.'

Nina rubbed a hand up her arm, trying to ease the goose bumps that speckled her skin, and then lowered her voice.

'How close was it?'

'He almost made it,' Kyle murmured. 'If Larry hadn't made that call to his team, we'd have had no hope.'

'Good God.'

'No such thing.' His mouth curved. 'Ah, before I forget. I need something back from you.'

'From me?'

Nina frowned as he leaned forward, wrapped his fingers around her arm, and turned her so she was facing away from him.

She gasped as his fingers moved from her arm to the back pocket of her jeans and reached inside.

She spun round, confused. 'What are you doing?'

His mouth quirked, and he held up a memory card. 'I need to take this with me.'

Nina stared at him, confused, before she realized what he had done. 'Wait a minute – while we were on the motorbike?'

He grinned and remained silent.

'You – you *planted* that on me?'

'It's safe, isn't it?'

Nina realized her mouth was hanging open and clamped her lips together, fury rising through her veins as she imagined what Hudson would have done to her if he'd found the card on her. 'You bastard.' She shook her head and changed the subject. 'What's on it?'

Kyle stopped laughing and held up the memory card between his fingers. 'It's a copy of the records Hudson kept for his business. His unofficial business, not the farm. Seems his paranoia extended to the people he was dealing with, so he kept records in case he was ever caught.' He lowered the card and frowned. 'John hid it in the door panel of the pick-up truck for safe-keeping when we escaped.'

Nina reached out and touched his arm. 'It's his legacy, Kyle. Make sure you take care of it now.'

He nodded, tucking the card into the pocket of his jeans before his gaze found hers, a twinkle in his eyes.

Nina pulled at her sleeves and glanced down at her muddy clothes, then noticed he was trying not to laugh. 'I look a state, don't I?'

A smile began to twitch at his mouth. 'I didn't say a

word.' He cleared his throat. 'But I don't think that look is going to take off in fashionable circles this year.'

She aimed a playful punch at his arm, before stopping, her fist in mid-air, when she saw him flinch.

'Sorry – I forgot. You seem to cope with being hurt so easily.'

Sadness flickered across his eyes.

'Only the physical stuff,' he said. 'I heal fast in that department.'

Nina bit her lip, wondering what, or who, had hurt Kyle so much in his past. Her thoughts were interrupted by a shout from the helicopter.

They both turned to see the pilot waving from his window, urging his passenger to hurry.

'Looks like I'm wanted,' said Kyle.

'Will I see you again?'

He smiled down at her. 'Maybe.' He held his hand up to the pilot at another shout from the aircraft. 'I meant to say,' he said, 'Ross has been transferred to Sacramento hospital. They're going to operate on his leg straight away, but they reckon he's going to be all right.'

Nina wiped her eyes before taking a deep breath. 'What's the story with you two? Are you going to tell me?'

He sighed and pointed over to the helicopter. 'Walk over with me. I'll tell you what I can.'

Nina fell into step with him, her heart hammering.

As they walked towards the helicopter, her boots sank into the waterlogged earth. She pulled the dark-blue FBI jacket around her shoulders, hugging it closer to her body, the fleece lining helping to alleviate the cool breeze that whipped across the empty paddock.

A mist had begun to rise, giving the landscape a grey, washed-out pallor. Dark silhouettes moved along the tree line between the aircraft and the smouldering ruins of the ranch.

Nina stumbled, fatigue slowly taking over her body, the adrenaline of the past few hours subsiding, and Kyle reached out to steady her and then began to explain.

'After my field office got a call from Ross twelve months ago he started sending them regular updates about Hudson's activities while a plan to expose him was developed,' he said. 'I started building my cover story six months ago.' He chuckled. 'I could never have known at the time it'd lead to something like this.' He gestured to the ruined buildings.

'I–I never knew,' said Nina. 'He never said anything to me. Not once over the past three days.'

Kyle shrugged. 'I don't think he wanted to scare you. He probably thought if he helped you patch up the truck stop and get it ready for sale that you'd be out of here before anything bad happened.' He reached up and tucked a loose strand of hair behind her ear. 'He cares a lot about his family – and friends.'

Nina bit her lip, unable to speak as tears welled in her eyes.

The federal agent leaned forward and kissed her on the

cheek, his days-old stubble scratching her skin, before he turned and jogged to the helicopter and climbed into the cockpit next to the pilot.

He grinned at her and shouted over the noise of the engine.

'Be good, Nina O'Brien. I'll be seeing you.'

FORTY

Nina flicked the page of the paperback novel she'd been trying to concentrate on, gave up, and flung it onto the low table next to the hard plastic chair.

Before leaving Hudson's property, Kyle had pulled some strings and arranged for her and Ross's brother to fly to Sacramento with two other agents in a second helicopter so they could be at the hospital when Ross awoke from the anaesthetic.

Friends of Ross's from Mistake Creek had stayed at the farm, organising the hired help to provide food and hot drinks for the emergency services and federal agents who were tearing apart what was left of their neighbour's property.

Ross's surgeon had appeared an hour ago, told her the operation to repair Ross's leg had gone well, and that he would make a full recovery over time with plenty of physiotherapy.

Nina had slumped exhaustedly into the chair to wait for Tim to return from the room next door where he'd commandeered a spare desk phone to contact all Ross's friends to assure them he was going to be okay.

When he did, he dropped into the chair next to Nina's and leaned forward, balancing his elbows on his knees.

'How are they getting on?'

'They're fine. I think they're glad to be busy – keeps their minds off what could have happened,' he said. He rubbed his neck and then leaned back in his chair. 'Any news?'

'Not yet.'

The teenager reached out and squeezed her hand. 'Hang in there, okay?'

She nodded, hearing his voice break, and squeezed back. 'I will. You too.'

He let go, shuffled in his seat, and seemed to consider his words before speaking.

'You can tell me this is none of my business, but why did you leave, all those years ago?'

Nina began to chew a nail and then lowered her hand. 'Tim, trust me – in hindsight I knew I shouldn't have done.'

'Did Ross hurt you?'

'No!' She was shocked. 'No, Ross would never hurt

me.' She looked down at her hands. 'I just misinterpreted what our friendship was. It was my fault.'

'Oh.'

He fell silent, waiting for her to continue, but she was saved by the appearance of a doctor, who shook hands with them both.

'He's heavily medicated,' he explained, 'but you can go in and see him now.'

Nina followed Tim along the corridor, then through a door to a private room, the city lights blinking through the window in the night sky.

'Hey.' Ross's face broke into a sleepy smile when he saw them. 'I wondered where you were.'

Nina couldn't contain the sob that burst from her lips. She ran to the bed, crouched down, and wrapped her hands around his.

'I thought I'd lost you forever,' she whispered when she could speak. 'I was so scared.'

When she drew back, Ross wiped his eyes.

'I didn't know what to do when I saw you and Kyle on the back of that motorbike,' he said. 'Then, when Sean appeared with my rifle, I thought he was going to kill me.'

He explained about faking his gut shot wound, then the couple's decision to leave him.

'Good job the gas was pumped from the tanks, too,' he said, telling Nina about their attempts to destroy the truck stop.

'What happened?'

'I was terrified,' said Ross. 'I knew he'd come back to kill me. I heard the car door slam and then remembered the nail-gun next to the toolbox by the counter.'

He fell silent, and Nina held his hand, guessing what had happened next.

'What did the police say?'

His lips pursed. 'They were going to arrest me.' He shook his head to silence her. 'I killed a man, Nina. They were doing their job.' He shuffled, easing himself up to a sitting position. 'It turns out Kyle spoke to them, though, and explained the situation. I'm not being charged – they've agreed it was self-defence.'

'So, you phoned the police after you'd killed Sean?'

'No,' he said. 'I'd already managed to get as far as the phone.' His eyes met hers. 'I think I may have been a bit hysterical by the time I got through to a dispatcher who listened to me, and then Sean turned up. They heard everything.'

Nina sniffled at the thought of Ross having to drag himself through the building while in so much pain.

'You saved our lives,' she said, clutching his hand, tracing her fingers over his.

He squeezed her hand in reply.

When he didn't speak, Nina glanced up to see him watching her intently. She bit her lip.

'Ross? I have to ask – are you with the FBI as well?'

A smile twitched at the corner of his mouth before he spoke.

'I'd love to sound really tough and say yes,' he said. 'But no, I'm not.'

'Then why did you get involved?'

He shrugged. 'It was the right thing to do,' he explained. 'Hudson always kept to himself, never socialized or anything, so when Tim and I saw vehicles coming and going, and different people milling around the place, we decided to keep an eye on the place. When we found out about the drugs, we reported it.' He sighed. 'I never imagined it'd come to this – or that it wasn't even about the drugs.'

'Do you want to go and work for the FBI?'

He snorted and then fell silent, and his face clouded over. He gripped her fingers between his.

'No, I don't,' he said quietly. 'All I ever wanted was for everything to be back how it used to be around here.' He rubbed at his eyes. 'No chance of that now, with Dad gone.'

'Ross, I'm so sorry.' She squeezed his hand. 'I think, in his heart, he believed he was somehow doing the right thing to keep a home for you two. I don't think he knew about all of Hudson's plans until it was too late.'

Nina turned to see Tim watching them, saying nothing.

'How badly damaged is the truck stop?' she asked. 'Did they tell you? Do I want to know?'

Tim rubbed his hand over his chin. 'They say there's a fair bit of damage,' he said. 'Mostly from the wind – you know about the front window, but some of the roofing on the accommodation block is loose.'

Nina stood and walked over to the window, peering down at the cars moving like toys on the intersection below.

'I'll have to move back here and oversee the repairs,' she said. 'And that could take me weeks.'

'Well,' said Tim, 'you might want to reconsider that.'

'What do you mean?' said Nina, frowning when she saw the teenager smile.

'I took the liberty of asking the police to check your father's insurance papers,' he explained. 'You're covered for all the damage, which should give you a head start. And we're getting a lot of enquiries from the media about accommodation in the area while they cover the story.' He shrugged. 'Apart from that, there's nothing that can't be sorted out with a few hands on deck and a couple of days' hard work,' he said. 'I'm more than happy to help you, if you'd like me to.'

Nina's heart began to pound as the realisation of what he was suggesting hit her, and she moved back to where Ross lay.

She'd be able to get the truck stop up and running again. Bring her father back from the city, home to Mistake Creek.

'What do you think, Nina?' asked Ross, reaching out and squeezing her hand. 'Do you want to come home for a while? It would be good to spend some time with you and catch up.'

'You promise you won't make me listen to country and western music while I'm there?'

He laughed. 'I promise.'

Nina wiped the tears from her eyes and smiled. 'Then, yes. Yes, I do.'

FORTY-ONE

Six weeks later

Nina shielded her eyes and peered at the horizon.

Beyond the trees that surrounded the back of the property, the main highway ran in a straight line for another half mile or so before it curved to the left and out of sight. Small clouds of dust curled in the breeze, while a black crow picked at the carcass of a small mammal to the side of the scarred asphalt. She squinted in the fading light, the sun now a thin golden line at the horizon while the sky above flared orange and purple against the vista of fresh crops and scrubby trees.

The valley had blossomed since the drought-breaking storm drenched the community, and farmers who had once contemplated moving away from the land were now reestablishing themselves – and attracting investment from outside the agriculture sector.

The news coverage of hers and Ross's involvement in preventing a major terrorism attack hadn't hurt either, with a number of journalists and television crews visiting the area to interview them during the weeks since. Although the incursion into their lives had been brief, it had put Mistake Creek back on the map.

The truck stop had entered a new phase too. The sudden influx of tourists to the area, traveling through the valley after hearing the story, and later in order to reach the blossoming national parks at either end of the valley, were taking full advantage of the easy access to fuel and overnight accommodation.

Nina crossed the forecourt, carrying a pack of soft drinks to restock one of the refrigerators next to the front counter. The income from the truck stop was now more than enough to fund her father's decision to retire to a small house in Mistake Creek and leave the running of the business to her while she organized a sale. Dealing with the contractors she'd engaged to renovate the truck stop and accommodation block at least gave her a focus. Despite abandoning her search for a city job without a backward glance, Nina was at a loss what to do next with her life.

Meanwhile, Ross had settled into the running of his father's farm, he and Tim splitting the profit they would now realize by the end of the year.

Despite being eager for a sale, Nina was grateful for the extra time she'd been able to stay in Mistake Creek, as it had enabled her to spend time with the two Flanagans and reignite the friendship she'd had with them ten years ago.

They were easy to get on with, and she'd spent many evenings in the farm kitchen listening avidly to Ross's plans. He was even contemplating taking over Hudson's abandoned land once the federal authorities were finished with their investigation.

She looked over her shoulder at the sound of a lone motorbike traveling along the road towards her and then frowned as it drew closer, her heartbeat clawing at her chest.

Surely not.

Hadn't Sean been killed by Ross?

What was he doing back here?

The motorbike slowed, indicated, and then executed a sweeping turn, stopping under the shade of the canopy.

The rider pulled off his helmet, his hair spiky and a broad grin plastered across his face.

'Kyle!'

Nina dropped the pack of soft drinks onto the step and hurried over to him.

He laughed as he swung a leg over the bike and enveloped her in his arms. 'Look at you! My God – how busy are you?'

Nina pulled away and looked over her shoulder at the

fresh timber window frames and bright signage that adorned the building.

'Luckily, I've had some help.'

'It's looking good,' Kyle said. He pushed his sunglasses onto his head as his gaze dropped to meet hers. 'So are you.'

'What are you doing back here?' asked Nina.

He cleared his throat and avoided her eye. 'I'm on extended leave.'

'Oh. Is that a good thing? I thought you lived for your job?'

'Yeah, well,' he said, and scratched at his earlobe. 'Let's just say they suggested I take a break after finding out I don't cope well being cooped up in an office.' He sighed. 'The operation's being scrutinized, Nina. Even though we stopped Hudson, my partner was killed.'

'I'm sorry, Kyle. You're good at what you do.' She reached out and put her hand on his arm. 'You'll be reinstated, though, right?' She frowned as his eyes met hers. 'Or is it more serious?'

The familiar quirk at the side of his mouth twitched. 'You could say that.'

'Won't your bosses want you back?'

'We're not exactly on speaking terms at the moment.'

'Oh.' Nina blushed. She glanced at the motorbike. 'Where are you going?'

'I thought I'd see where the road takes me. Then I

changed my route and cut through here. I figured I'd see how you were getting on before I head east.'

'Well, I'd better sort you out with some gas; otherwise you won't be going far.'

She moved towards the bowser, waited while Kyle opened the cap of the fuel tank, and then began to fill it.

He peered over her shoulder. 'Looks like the business is doing well.'

'It is doing well.' She turned and ran her gaze over the neatly landscaped garden beds leading back to the refurbished accommodation block.

'What happened? I thought you weren't going to stay here?'

Nina shrugged. 'I'm not, but after everything broke on the news about the terrorist threat and how the FBI had managed to stop the truck, the media were here for weeks,' she said. 'Mistake Creek finally made it back onto the map. After the television crews and everybody else paid to stay here while they covered the story, I had enough money to renovate.' She turned back to Kyle. 'Once they'd gone, the tourists started coming back. It's been amazing. The truck stop goes on the market next week, and hopefully we'll make enough to give Dad a comfortable retirement.'

'And Ross?'

'Taking his time getting well,' she said. 'He had to have weeks of physiotherapy.' She sighed. 'It wasn't easy, but it was while he was recovering and I was staying at his family's house helping him that we realized we'd never be more than friends.'

She saw a frown crease his brow, then lift as she spoke.

'It's nice, though,' she added. 'It's been great seeing what he and Tim have got planned for the farm.' She looked down as the bowser stopped. 'All done. You'll be able to clear a few more hundred miles now.'

'Great, thanks.' He reached into his pocket.

'I'm not taking your money, Kyle,' said Nina. She ran her gaze over the motorbike. 'So, how did you end up with this?'

Kyle shrugged. 'Every now and again, the police auction off goods seized from criminals – the money goes towards funding local youth clubs and the like.' He patted the seat. 'I thought I could give it a good home.'

'Wait,' said Nina. 'I'll get some food for you to take with you.'

After Nina had dashed into the truck stop, she took a second to gather her thoughts, her mind racing as she packed a bag with food and soft drinks.

He said he'd ridden out to see how she was doing. And that it was unlikely he had a job anymore. And he was heading east.

She swallowed. What if she never saw him again?

She sealed the bag, and rushed back through the building, but when she returned to the forecourt, Kyle was sitting on the bike, ready to go.

She handed over the supplies and watched him stuff them into his sports bag fastened to the seat behind him.

'At least you won't starve for a few days,' she said, trying to remain calm, to sound cheerful.

Kyle winked. 'Thanks. I appreciate it.' He surprised her by pulling her into a hug. 'You're a tough one, Nina O'Brien,' he murmured, his voice raw. 'I couldn't stop thinking about you.'

He kissed her cheek, his stubble lightly scratching against her skin, a faint trace of his cologne clinging to her as he let her go.

Nina stepped back as he started the motorbike, the engine roaring to life. She shivered, the memories of that stormy night briefly returning before she blinked back the tears that suddenly filled her eyes and swallowed to clear the pain in her throat before speaking.

'Why don't you stay here?'

He frowned, unable to hear her over the engine. 'What?'

She tried again, her voice louder, unable to prevent the tremor that accompanied her words.

'Stay here.'

'Here?'

'I could use some help.' She saw his Adam's apple bob in his throat and realized he was as nervous as she felt.

She couldn't let him disappear from sight again. The thought of Kyle Roberts riding that damned motorbike off into the distance forever was too painful.

She pointed at the new timber, then the walls of the building. 'I could use a hand with the painting, and it gets really busy here at weekends with tourists driving through the valley…,' she said, and then fell silent, scared that she'd sounded too desperate, too eager to make him stay.

She realized he was watching her intently, and then he reached out and killed the motorbike engine, its rumble falling silent.

He kicked the stand to the ground, then climbed from the bike, pulled off his gloves and tossed them onto the saddle.

She trembled as he stalked towards her, but she held her chin up and tried not to cross her arms over her chest. She'd forgotten how imposing he could be.

As he drew closer, she wondered if she'd read him wrong, whether she'd been mistaken about the spark that she'd felt between them. Her heart thumped painfully, and she ignored the sudden tightness in her chest.

And then he was standing in front of her, his blue eyes piercing.

'I thought you'd never ask,' he murmured, and pulled her into his embrace.

'You scared me,' she mumbled into his chest, inhaling his aroma. 'I thought you were going to leave forever.'

He pulled back, his hands on her arms as he stared at her. 'I couldn't,' he said, and then sighed. 'I'm tired, Nina. I'm tired of living like I have been. I'm tired of spending most of my days scared that I'm turning into someone I hate. I'm tired of always being on the wrong side of right.'

'What *do* you want?' Nina whispered.

'I want to be with you,' he said, his mouth so close to her she could feel his breath on her cheek. 'Apart from that, I don't care where I am in the world.'

He kissed her and then rested his chin against her head as he peered up at the truck stop. 'So, are you going to give me the guided tour?'

'Okay.' She waited while he bent down and picked up the carton of soft drinks she'd dropped to the ground. 'What do you want to see first?'

He chuckled, and Nina felt her legs weaken. 'You'd better show me where you keep the paintbrushes.'

He winked and led the way across the forecourt towards the front door, holding it open for her.

Nina laughed and led him into the truck stop, then turned the sign on the door to 'Closed'.

THE END

ABOUT THE AUTHOR

Before turning to writing, USA Today bestselling crime author Rachel Amphlett played guitar in bands, worked as a TV and film extra, dabbled in radio, and worked in publishing as an editorial assistant.

She now wields a pen instead of a plectrum and writes crime fiction with over 30 crime novels and short stories featuring spies, detectives, vigilantes, and assassins.

A keen traveller, Rachel has both Australian and British citizenship.

You can find out more about Rachel and her books at www.rachelamphlett.com.

Lightning Source UK Ltd.
Milton Keynes UK
UKHW041040191022
410727UK00004B/215